Buckshot and the Boy

Buckshot and the Boy

A Classic Modern Cowboy Novelette

Merry Christmas to The Haines family — Hope you enjoy this story — Best wishes
Pete Hilgartner 2006

By Peter "Highpockets" Hilgartner

with

Kirsten J. Boyd

To order additional copies of this book, contact:
Xlibris Corporation
1-888-795-4274
www.Xlibris.com
Orders@Xlibris.com
33321-3

DEDICATION

To the memory of Herman and Becky Sparks,

and to my brothers, both called "Tex" by their friends

Fielding P. and Lee M. Hilgartner,

without whose influence and love my life would have never been the same.

BUCKSHOT AND THE BOY
STORY SUMMARY

This is a classic fictional cowboy story written for young adults in a dynamic style. The intricate fabric of this tale surrounds the life and adventures of a 1938 teenage boy. Because his father considers him to be a problem, he farms his son out to a Southwest Texas rancher.

At the ranch, the boy receives responsibilities. The work is physically tough. He is given opportunities to excel in situations that are sometimes stressful and sometimes humorous. The high standards set, along with good leadership and love provided by the rancher and his wife prevail. The surprise ending is especially moving.

Backshot and the Boy

January 8, 2006

A 'By the Oak' Original

$$1$$

The two of them stood about eight feet apart looking each other straight in the eye. The boy was not smiling; his face was a combination of resentment and uncertainty. He was squinting with the right eye partially closed. The boy was *not* happy! The man, who stood at just less than six feet in his worn cowboy boots, had a slight grin on his weather-beaten suntanned face. The man spoke first. "I'm Jesse Steel, and I'll be taking you down to our ranch. Your father told you all this, right?"

"Yes sir," the boy replied mechanically. There was no trust in his voice. "Yesterday was my last day of school. He told me to pack my gear, and you'd be coming to get me. Where are we going?" he asked.

"My ranch is located about 30 miles from La Flor, near the mountains between the Nueces River and the Rio Grande River. We have a long day before us, so we'd better get started."

The boy scuffed his feet in the dirt, and watched the dust cover his worn shoes. "How long will it take?"

"It'll take all day, probably eight hours from Austin. We'd better load up and get going."

The man put the lad's suitcase into the old black Model A Ford, as the boy climbed carefully into the front seat. He started the engine and they were underway. It had turned into a blistering hot 1938 June day with hardly a cloud in the sky as the old car chugged along. The sun was almost at its midday apex when they reached San Antonio. Here they stopped at a country store with gas pumps for a fill up and to stretch their legs.

"Your father give you any money?" the man asked, wiping the sweat off his forehead as he began filling the gas tank.

"He gave me ten dollars," the boy answered.

"Well, you'd better get a soda or something and a sandwich or hot dog. Mrs. Steel will feed us after we arrive home, but that won't be for a while yet."

Other than this brief conversation, very few words had been exchanged between them. As they left the country store, the man turned off the main highway and headed west on a much narrower road. They were now headed due west facing into the sun.

The man knew little about the boy except that his father considered him a 'problem' and said the boy's behavior had become less than tolerable. After considerable pressure from his wife, the stepmother, the boy's father had decided to collect on a debt Jesse Steel owed him, but could not pay. In order to settle the debt, the men reached an agreement. Steel would take the boy for at least six months and the debt would be erased. The boy knew nothing of this. He despised his father, and to him anywhere would be better than living in his father's home.

Steel was mulling the situation over in his mind during the drive to San Antonio. The boy was very thin, scared, and obviously distrusted him. They were driving directly into the sun now. Steel had pulled the only visor down to shade his eyes. He looked over and noticed the boy working hard to shade his own eyes, first with his hands, then by turning his face to one side or the other. His discomfort was obvious; he sat up very straight with his back barely touching the seat.

"If you'll put your cap on you'll find it helps to shade your eyes better," said the man.

"Don't have a hat" replied the youth.

"Well, there's a store up ahead. We'll stop there and get one."

He turned the car into the parking spot of a small but tidy looking yellow storefront. The two got out and walked into the building together.

"Got any caps that will fit this boy?" Steel asked the owner, a short weathered fellow with a scraggly beard.

"All we got here is some straw sombreros and cowpoke hats. We also have some baseball caps. They're all five dollars apiece."

"Kid, I don't think you'd look so good in a baseball cap. Tell you what," Steel turned to the storekeeper "This one's on me—find a hat that will fit this lad so we can get moving again. And if you don't mind, throw in a soda for him too."

The storekeeper smiled, showing yellow stained teeth, and in short order the boy had a proper straw cowboy hat with a brim that would serve him well in shading his eyes and protecting him from the sun.

When they returned to the vehicle and had climbed in, Steel turned to look at his passenger. There was a glimmer of a smile on the boy's face. The boy seemed to hesitate, then asked his first question.

"How much further do we have to go?"

"We should get there just about sundown." Steel replied. "When we get home Mrs. Steel will be expecting me to introduce you right proper. What name do you go by at your home, Jacob Leroy, Jacob or Leroy?"

"I hate those names," snapped the boy, "those are my father's names. I don't like Junior either."

"Well, what shall I call you?" he asked, smiling at the boy's first sign of gumption.

"You can call me Jake, Jake Hall," said the boy proudly. "That's what my mother calls me."

"OK, Jake it'll be, and you can call me Mr. Steel for now" said Jesse Steel with a smile.

Although Jake didn't realize this, bonding between the man and the boy had begun in a small way. They were getting close to the ranch when Jake turned and asked bluntly, "Is Mrs. Steel pretty? Does she have rules?"

"Jake, you can decide for yourself on her looks." Jesse choked back a laugh. "Yes, there will probably be some special things Mrs. Steel will ask us to do, like washing hands and being on time for meals. Most of the 'rules' set by Mrs. Steel will apply to both of us."

"What about baths?" Jake asked, adjusting his position on the car seat.

Steel laughed, "She'll let you know," he replied. "We're getting close. Got any more questions?"

"Yes sir," Jake said, "Do you have any children?"

"No, not anymore. Our young son died some time ago" he replied sadly. Jake knew immediately that this was not a topic for further discussion, so he paused, then asked, "What kind of ranch do you have, Mr. Steel?"

"Well," Steel replied, "we have a small ranch with a little bit of everything on it. You'll find out soon enough."

He turned the car onto a gravel road saying, "We're now on the ranch property. It's only a short distance to the gate." He stopped the car at the gate and Jake noticed that it was very unique in its structure. A ten foot pole stood in the center of the gateway, from which the gate was mounted. The center of the gate itself was mounted on this post. From the top of the pole two large cables were secured, each end stretching to a gate end. Pieces of old tires were tied to the gate, engineered so that the car bumper would push them, allowing the gate to swing open and the car to pass through. On top of the pole was the skull of a long-horned steer. This gate and its operation was something Jesse Steel had designed and Jake could tell he was proud of it.

The ranch house was not large, but it was well cared for. Its green shutters stood out nicely against the white walls. A small white picket fence surrounded the house and allowed an ample exercise area for a tan and white dog that was barking furiously as the car stopped in front of the gate. On the front porch stood a pleasant looking woman wearing a blue gingham dress with a white apron. Jake noted some streaks of grey in her dark brown hair.

Mrs. Steel came down the steps smiling and gave her husband a big hug as he came through the gate. Jake remained in the car.

Jesse smiled. "Come on, boy! Get on out of the car so you can meet the Mrs."

Jake exited cautiously and retrieved his bag from the rear seat.

"Betsy, hold onto Snickers till we've introduced him to Jake, please." said Steel pointing to the jumping dog. "Jake, this lady is my wife. Betsy, this here's Jake."

"We are so happy to have you, Jake" said Mrs. Steel as she tried to give Jake a hug. As she did this the boy winced and jumped away from her, his eyes misting up. The two adults looked surprised but said nothing. Jesse Steel frowned. Something was wrong here and it set him to thinking.

At dinner Jake ate pretty well. He was hungry, but picky.

"Well, he's just nervous," Mrs. Steel thought, "He does have nice manners." She liked his ramrod posture at the table. His back didn't touch the back of the chair once during the entire meal.

After dinner Mrs. Steel gave Jake a tour of the house, which was a simple rectangular structure. The front of the house faced west. On the right, or south side of the house were two bedrooms, with a bathroom squeezed in between. The bathroom could be entered from the back bedroom occupied by the Steels. The bathroom also had a second door that provided entry from the family 'sitting' room, and could be accessed by the occupant of the front bedroom via the same room. There was no formal dining room. A table had been placed behind the sofa in the sitting room and was set back enough to accommodate four chairs.

The kitchen, on the east side of the house, was the last room Jake visited. A door led to the small screened in porch at the back of the house. A clothes line was attached just outside the door and extended to a post some distance into the backyard. This yard was fairly large and had two gates, one on the north side and the other at the east end of the yard. Even though the sun had already set, Jake was able to get a pretty good idea of his new home.

As they re-entered the kitchen from the porch, Mrs. Steel smiled and said, "Jake, you've seen our home now. The front bedroom will be yours. Let's go into the sitting room and join Jesse." Jake noticed as they walked to the sitting room that the kitchen possessed a very uncommon item, a refrigerator. As they toured the house Jake could tell Mrs. Steel was very happy to own this luxury item.

Sitting with the Steels was a very quiet affair. It was an evening ritual they kept after dinner. Both were avid readers. Mrs. Steel, a former school teacher, was employed as a librarian until she met Jesse. After the death of their son, the evening ritual became even more important to them, and the Bible was the book of choice.

Jake sat on the edge of a chair looking around for something to read, but found nothing of interest. He sat, twiddling his thumbs and wondering if he should say anything. He was tired from the long trip and his back was still aching. Finally, Mrs. Steel looked up and broke the silence.

"You look tired, boy, why don't you go wash up and get ready for bed. We'll come in shortly and bid you goodnight."

Jake gratefully went to his room and began to undress.

June in southwest Texas can be very hot. Temperatures hovered near the 100 degree mark. There was no such thing as 'air conditioning' in 1938 Ranch homes, at least on the Steel's "S Arrow" ranch. Despite the heat, Jake's eyelids became heavier and heavier as he flopped on his stomach and soon fell fast asleep.

After giving Jake some time to get settled, the Steels decided to go and say goodnight to the boy. Mrs. Steel thought she'd say a bedtime prayer along with their goodnight. To their surprise, they found Jake sound asleep.

"Jesse," Betsy whispered, "he didn't take a bath. What are these spots on the back of his shirt?" She pointed to Jake's shirt which was draped over a chair.

"Look at his back," whispered Jesse, "it appears he's had a pretty stout whipping."

He pointed to the welts etched across the boy's back. Several had scabbed up but a couple had broken open and leaked blood onto his shirt during the long trip.

"No wonder he sat up so straight at suppertime", Mrs. Steel said.

"I wondered why he was fidgeting so in the car on the trip down. Let's leave him be for tonight," said her husband.

"There must be something wrong with this boy's father." Betsy commented, "He must be sick or an alcoholic or something! How could a father do such thing? The boy's back looks like it's been horse whipped!"

The Steels went to the most private place in their house—their bedroom, to discuss the situation.

"Oh, Jesse," Betsy said with tears in her eyes, "I was so happy when we learned about Jake's coming. Tommy would have been about his same age now and I've missed him terribly."

"I know," said Jesse softly, "I've missed Tommy as much as you have but we have a new boy now, a 'problem child' I was told. It looks like we have, in fact, an abused boy, one who could use some love. I agree with you, there must be something wrong with the father. I know from talking with him that he has a temper! I don't believe this lad is the problem. I believe his father is the culprit."

"Well," Betsy responded, "maybe we can help this boy. Anyway, time will tell! I know you can help. I love you, and believe in you," she whispered.

"I'll do my best to help this boy, and I love you too," he answered.

2

The next day it rained all day. The storm came up suddenly in the wee hours of the morning as storms often do in Texas. When Jake awoke, he realized someone had covered him with a sheet. He could smell bacon cooking in the kitchen, and he heard Mr. Steel's footsteps at the back door. "My, it's wet out there!" Jake heard him say as he stamped his feet. "Thankfully the rest of the animals are OK! It looks like a fox got one of our chickens. Where's old sleepy head, still in the bunk? Hey boy, you up yet?" He called out.

Jake came in the kitchen, barefoot but with the same white shirt on he had worn the day before, only the shirttail was hanging down over his worn pants. "It's a mess out there," Steel said, as he shook the water out of his hair, to Betsy's chagrin. "You ready to chow down, Jake?"

The two sat down to a meal of grits, bacon, fried eggs and cornbread. Steel had a big mug of black coffee and a glass of milk was poured for Jake. Mrs. Steel had already eaten and did not join them.

Jesse glanced at the boy. "Jake, today being Saturday, we usually drive to town so Mrs. Steel can shop. It's so nasty out, we'll probably just stay home today—if that's okay with you, Betsy."

"That's fine," she said, "I can manage till next Saturday. I've plenty to catch up on here. We've some bills to pay and I need to do a little bookkeeping."

It was obvious, even to Jake, that the adults were good people who worked together as a team. As they continued their meal, Jesse decided to do some probing and see if he could learn more about Jake.

"Jake, I would take you to the barns today and maybe ride out an' check on the herd in our north field, but it's too wet for that. You play any games son?"

"Yes sir," Jake looked hopeful. "I like checkers okay."

"What kind of sports do you like?"

"I like baseball okay, especially when I get to bat."

"Baseball, aye?" Now Steel looked hopeful.

"I haven't played a lot, but I like the infield better than the outfield. Being a right fielder is boring." Jake said bluntly.

"That's fine son," said Steel with a grin. "I've got a couple of mitts and if it clears up this afternoon maybe we can go outside and toss a few balls around or even pitch some horseshoes. You like that idea?"

"Both sound OK to me" Jake said as he squirmed around in his chair.

"Jesse, you mentioned the fox got one of our chickens," interjected Mrs. Steel "Before he gets any more, would you go out and catch up a couple of those fat roosters so I can fix them for supper?" She turned to the boy. "You like fried chicken, Jake?"

"Yes, ma'am!" The boy looked up quickly and with enthusiasm.

Mrs. Steel smiled. "While Jesse's out fetching the chickens would you help me fold up this wash and all?" She pointed to the large mound of clothes and sheets on a nearby couch.

"Yes ma'am!"

Mrs. Steel seated herself on one end of the couch, put the linens and wash in the middle and motioned for Jake to sit at the other end.

"Jake, last night after you went to sleep, we saw those welts on your back. Want to tell me about it?" She turned to the clothes, "Those welts will need a washing so they'll heal quickly."

Jake sat very still and said nothing.

"Jake, you can talk to me and Jesse." Mrs. Steel's voice softened. "We had a boy who died about five years ago. We don't know why, he just got sick and God took him back. While you're with us, we want to treat you as if you were our son. We need to be able to talk with each other when we have problems." She smiled tearfully. "That's what mothers and sons are supposed to do."

"Yes ma'am."

It took a while, but Betsy was finally able to get Jake to tell her what had happened. The previous Saturday evening his father and step-mother had gone out to a party. Jake had neglected to take a bath before heading to bed and he fell asleep instead with his clothes on. The next thing he knew he had been jerked out of bed, stripped of his clothes and thrown into a tub of water. After being yanked out of the tub he was subjected to a beating with a horse quirt.

Mrs. Steel listened to the boy's story, then looked him straight in the eye.

"Thank you Jake, for sharing your story with me. Know that Jesse and I will keep this to ourselves. However," she turned and her gray eyes brightened, "right now we need to get you and that back of yours cleaned and medicated. I'm sure you'll be fine in a few days." She resumed sorting the laundry. "Tomorrow is Sunday. Jesse and I would like to take you to church with us. We may just meet some folks you might like."

Sunday arrived, and after a quick breakfast the Steels began their preparations for church by putting on their 'Sunday go to meeting' clothes. Jake was duly spruced up in a clean shirt and blue jean trousers.

At church, Jake enjoyed listening to the hymns, but found the sermon thoroughly boring. The preacher spoke on Isaiah 58:9-14, verses on fasting, hypocrisy, keeping the Sabbath and becoming strong. Jake wasn't especially interested in the fasting part and knew he would only keep the Sabbath if the Steels took him to church. Jake missed the bigger picture however. He didn't realize that the words in verse 11 mirrored his needs to a tee. The deeper meaning of the verses did not escape the Steels. They glanced at each other in understanding. La Flor was a sun scorched land and from it came strong men and women. Jake would be rebuilt and become strong. Doing this would be their goal.

Following the service Jake accompanied the Steels to the meeting hall where some refreshments of cookies, coffee and lemonade were being served. A man and woman waved at the Steels from across the room, and walked over to greet them.

Jesse greeted them warmly, "Morning, Jim and Ruth, good to see you. Want you to meet my new 'hand' at the ranch." Mr. Steel gestured towards Jake. "This here is Jake Hall, the youngster I told you about who'd be staying with us for a while. Jake, this is Jim and Ruth Rivers. Ruth is Betsy's sister, and Jim and I have been friends for a long time. And where are Kathy and young Timmy?" he asked the couple.

"I think Timmy is outside with some of the young 'uns and Kathy. Oh, there she is!" Jim waved at Kathy as she came walking over to join her parents.

"Morning, Uncle Jesse and Aunt Betsy," she said politely "who is this with you?"

Jake was standing between the Steels as Kathy walked towards them. His eyes grew to the size of two saucers and his mouth hung ajar. This was not a girl—this was an angel, the loveliest creature he had ever seen. Jake was going on 14, that is, he would be fourteen in September. Kathy was a little older, 13 or maybe already 14. When she was introduced it was all he could do to say 'hi' and feebly wave his hand. Kathy looked him over, smiled, and quickly turned her head, flipping her long silky black hair in Jake's face. She spoke only to her mother and Aunt Betsy. Maybe this was a brush off, but all Kathy did was increase the palpitations in Jake's heart.

Jesse turned to Jake, "Mr. Rivers owns the hardware and feed store here in town. We usually stop by Rivers General Supply and Feed Store when we come to town. He sells just about everything a rancher might need except livestock and groceries!"

"Jake," Mr. Rivers turned to the boy, "You got a pocket knife?"

"No sir," the boy replied.

"Well next time you come to town, stop by. We just got in some new Barlow knives and they are dandy!"

Jake's eyes began to shine with anticipation.

3

The Sun had hardly shown itself on Monday morning when Jake heard a deep voice call out, "Wake, snakes, the day is a-breaking, the pea's in the pod and the hoecake's bakin'! Reveille boy! Time's a-wastin'!"

"Reveille? What's reveille?" The sleepy voice replied.

"If you were in the Marines, you'd know about reveille. Let's go. Up and at 'em!"

Jake slid over to the edge of the bed and sat up rubbing his eyes.

"We've got exciting things to do today, Jake, and I need an extra hand. Besides you haven't seen the place yet, and I want to show you around!"

At this invitation, Jake began dressing as fast as he could.

The breakfast was wonderful. Mrs. Steel had added toasted bread and syrup to the normal bacon and egg fare. Once outside with Jesse, Jake looked in the direction of the barns. Saddled and tied to the corral were two horses. One was a large grey horse and the other a smaller pinto. He noticed there was a shotgun in a scabbard attached to the saddle of the larger horse.

"Are we going riding today?" Jake asked.

"You bet!" was the enthusiastic answer. "The pinto will be yours to use while we're here. She's Betsy's favorite. Her name is Star for that white star-like mark on her forehead. She's about fourteen hands tall, a good cow pony. Come on over here: our hogs are in these two pens." Jesse gestured toward the pigs. "That big black hog over there is a wild one we roped and brought in here last winter. The fat black and white one is Matilda. She was born here and was the only piglet her mother produced. She's pretty gentle and loves carrots, apples and just about anything else."

Jake smiled at the mention of feeding treats to Matilda.

Jesse continued, "One of the chores I'm assigning you is to help me 'slop' these hogs each day. You can bring our table scraps and mix them with some feed and water, then pour the mix into those troughs." Jesse pointed to the wooden troughs "Just climb up on the fence, but don't fall in. That black boar will attack you and you could get hurt pretty badly. Doin' this right each time is very important; understand, son?"

"Yes sir." Jake answered "What happens to the pigs?"

"Some we sell, and each fall one or two are put down for our own use. That's where Mrs. Sparks gets all her bacon and ham. She also makes the best hogshead cheese you ever ate!"

Continuing on, Jesse pointed to two horses in another corral.

"Those are my other horses," he said. "The brown one is a pack and plow horse. The black one is my riding horse. He's fairly young, sixteen hands high and about five years old. He can be a little rambunctious at times."

"What are their names?" Jake asked

"My horses don't have fancy names," grinned Jesse "The gray is called "Grey", the black "Black" and the brown we call "Brownie" Pretty simple, no?"

"Easy to remember," observed the boy.

Jesse chuckled, "Well, let's get moving kid. You've ridden before, right?"

"Yes sir, plenty of times."

The morning was still and cool as they rode out to the north pasture, which held the Steel's small herd of about fifty white-faced cattle.

"This pasture has proven to be the best and only one we can keep cattle in" said Jesse. "It's so dry down here in the summer, even the little creek that cuts through the northeast corner of this pasture dries up. If it weren't for the windmills, we couldn't keep any cows up here."

They continued riding in a southwesterly direction towards some fairly steep hills.

"Our sheep are up there" said Jesse, pointing to the top of a ridge.

"Sheep!" Jake scoffed. "I thought you had a real ranch!" All the cowboy stories and Lone Ranger movies Jake had ever read or seen were about cowboys versus Indians and cattle wars by ranchers against sheep herders. At times he had daydreamed of being a dashing cowboy with a white Stetson hat, driving cattle north to St. Louis, fighting Indians and rescuing fair maidens in distress. His thoughts wandered back to Sunday and meeting Kathy. Maybe if he rescued her some day, she might like him too!

No, that will never happen—I'm not sure I even like her myself, thought Jake.

Jake noticed that Jesse had begun to move faster and had put his horse into a trot. Jake tried kicking Star, but she just kept plodding along. He took the reins, flipping the ends from side to side but with no better results. He took off his hat and began slapping the horse, which brought results immediately, as Star broke into a gallop. The suddenness of the increase in speed almost unsettled Jake as he reached for the pommel on the saddle, dropping his hat in the process. When horse and boy came alongside Steel, Jake said in a high voice, "Mr. Steel, I dropped my hat, can we go back and get it?"

They turned around and surprisingly Star led the way back—at a gallop nonetheless. Jake got her 'whoaed' as Steel rode up and grasped the pinto's reins. Jake dismounted and walked to retrieve his hat from among the rocks. Just as he was about to reach down and pick up the hat he heard an awful sound. Texas kids know the meaning of this particular burr, and Jake was no exception. "Brrrr-brrrr!" Jake looked frightened and he stopped with his hand inches from the hat.

"Freeze!" yelled Steel. A loud boom echoed through the hills. The firing of the shotgun not only sent the head of the big rattlesnake flying off into the air, but Jake managed about two feet of air space as well.

"Wow!" he exclaimed, after he regained some composure, "That was a great shot Mr. Steel! Gee, thanks!"

He was still shaking from the narrow escape, but Steel was grinning from ear to ear, "It's a good thing I was riding Grey today, Black would never have let me make a shot like that on him!"

"Why?" Jake inquired.

Steel reigned his horse beside Jake and continued, "Well, one time a city slicker came down here to hunt quail and I loaned him the black to ride. He asked me if it would be okay to shoot off the horse if he came upon a quail covey. I told him sure, it was okay to shoot *off* the horse. Well, we got onto a real nice covey and he fired his gun from atop the horse. The black reared and threw him off in a hurry! The man got up and yelled at me 'I thought you told me I could shoot off this horse!' I said 'I did, sir, but you shot while you were *on* the horse, not off of him!" Well, that ended that, and I never saw the man again. Black didn't like him and to tell the truth, neither did I, because from then on I had a gun-shy horse!"

By this time Jake was laughing heartily. He turned to look up at the man atop the gray horse. In his face there was a mixture of awe and wonder. To Jake, Jesse Steel was a god and this god now had a disciple.

The remainder of the ride up in the hills was uneventful. Steel had given Jake the trophy of trophies—ten rattles cut from the snake's tail now resided in Jake's pocket. The man and boy rode until just after they reached the plateau on the ridge top, where the sheep were quietly grazing. The lunch Mrs. Sparks made for them was unwrapped and wolfed down. Jake was full of questions, "How many sheep do you own, Mr. Steel? Why is that goat with the herd, and why does it have a bell around its neck?" Jesse began to chuckle.

"Slow down son. Being a sheep rancher is not easy. Sheep are stupid animals, which is why we have a goat. There are about 80 sheep in the herd. Our biggest worry is coyotes. That's why that dog you see is with the herd. Oscar is a sheep dog and his job is to stay with the herd all the time. Either you or I will need to ride up here on a daily basis to give him some chow. That's the only time he can leave the flock—when we feed him. There are a couple streams up here that drain into the creek we crossed through, so water is not a problem."

While inspecting the flock, Steel told Jake that he should look for screwworms in the side or neck of a sheep when he was inspecting the flock. If not treated promptly, the worms could create a large wound and quickly kill the sheep. Any wounds would be treated with a liquid called Benzol, followed by a tar like mixture called Pineoil. The sheep and even the cattle had to be inspected at least once a week as a precaution.

Jake couldn't wait to get back to the ranch house and tell Mrs. Steel about their adventures. They were both hot and dusty upon their return, but were cheerfully greeted by Mrs. Steel and a pitcher of cool water.

Jake began his story, "Mrs. Steel," the words came pouring out, "guess what happened? A big rattler was out there and when I went to get my hat, Mr. Steel shot him with a load of buckshot, just like real cowboys do!"

Mrs. Steel smiled, "Jesse is a real cowboy, don't you think?"

"Yes ma'am, he is, he's the best!"

Mrs. Steel was really beginning to enjoy this. Jesse left the room before Jake began his story, so she took the opportunity to say "Jake, you don't need to call me Mrs. Steel all the time. How about . . ." She started to say 'Mom' but checked herself. "How about . . . Aunt Betsy?"

"I'd like that ma'am, I mean, Aunt Betsy. But I don't think I want to call Mr. Steel 'Uncle Jesse'!"

"What would you like better?"

Jack wrinkled his nose in deep thought, "I think he should have a real cowboy name like, a name like . . . Buckshot! That's it! Buckshot! Like the shot he used to destroy that snake!"

"Well, here comes Jesse now. Let's see what he thinks about this." Betsy turned her pretty face towards Jesse, "Jesse, I've asked Jake to call me Aunt Betsy from now on and he's picked a name for you that he'd like to use."

Jesse looked interested. "What is it?"

"Jake, you tell him!"

"Mr. Steel, can I call you Buckshot? It's a real cowboy name and I think you're a real cowboy!" Jake spoke quickly then held his breath in anticipation.

"Son, you know what—I'd be real proud if you called me that. It's a deal. You know what else, I don't care much for the name you picked for yourself either. We call young male turkeys Jakes! You don't look much like a turkey to me. How about I call you 'Little Tex'? We cowboys need to stick together."

The next Sunday at church in La Flor, the Rivers met some old faces with new names, Aunt Betsy, Buckshot and Little Tex. The names stuck, especially Jesse's. He became known throughout all of La Flor as 'Buckshot' Steel.

4

June was passing quickly. Buckshot concentrated on fence repairs and improvements to the corrals. Tex was with him constantly, holding the other end when needed. Slowly, the scope of his chores increased, including the responsibility of grooming the horses and cleaning the stalls. Buckshot became the consummate teacher, but he also understood the importance of having some recreation at the end of the day. He made certain to include some time for fun or other pleasantry such as storytelling. As a result, he found Tex a willing and cooperative worker and student.

One day Buckshot asked, "Tex, how would you like to go shooting with me this afternoon?"

The boy's eyes widened, "You bet I would!"

"Well, I have an old single shot 20 gauge shotgun I think you can handle and we'll set some bottles up on yonder fence for you to shoot. We can start after we finish fixing this chute and loading ramp for the cattle. This will make it quick and easy to load the cows into the trucks.

The boy smiled. He had taken off his shirt and Buckshot observed that his back was completely healed. He also noticed some new muscles developing in the lad's slight frame. I do believe he's put on a couple of pounds, he thought.

Target practice that afternoon was a big success. Buckshot used the opportunity to teach and explain that knowing how to handle the gun safely was as important as good marksmanship. Tex took to the instruction like a duck to the water.

After supper they both moved into the sitting room for the evening Bible reading. When they finished Tex said, "Thanks, Buckshot, for the shooting lesson today. That was sure fun!" He was quiet for a moment then asked, "Buckshot, have you ever had any bad guys come onto the property, and do rustling or things like that?"

"Well son, as a matter of fact we have." Buckshot leaned back in his chair, a signature move indicating he was about to tell a story.

Betsy smiled, "Yes, tell him about what happened last November."

"Well," Buckshot began, "I decided to go deer hunting one morning. I got Black and Brownie ready the evening before and rode them out well before dawn to set up in a ridge just above the north pasture fence line. I staked the horses on the back side of the ridge and walked over to where I had a good view of the stream and the ranch house to my left. I could even see the ridge at the south end where our sheep usually graze. Not long after sunrise, I heard some shots coming from the south ridge. None of my friends would have been up there without contacting me first, so I thought it might be poachers. I ran back to the horses and rode lickity-split towards the house. Betsy had also heard the shots and was on the front porch when I arrived."

"I heard those shots and was very concerned," interjected Betsy. "I saw Jesse coming from the kitchen window, so I ran out to see if I could be of help. He told me to tie up Brownie and call Sheriff Mitchell. I tried to convince Jesse not to go up there alone, but he wouldn't listen. After tying up Brownie, I put a saddle on Grey so the Sheriff could use a fresh horse if he needed one. I was sure he would."

Buckshot continued, "Blackie moved out nicely for me. It didn't take long for us to reach the base of the ridge. As we started up the trail to the top, I heard the dogs barking and a couple more shots. By this time, I had my rifle in my hands, ready to use if necessary. Then I did a foolish thing. I should have dismounted, and sneaked up to the ridge using the rocks and trees for cover. Unfortunately I just charged right up over the hill. I saw them first, two of them. Two banditos! A couple of sheep were down and so was my dog, old Zero. They turned to shoot at me, but I got my shot off first. Blackie reared and went over on her side. Fortunately, I got my leg free before we hit the dirt. We came down hard and I hit my head on a rock. When I came to, the banditos were gone and so were the hindquarters of both sheep. Zero was dead, but Oscar had come back and was whimpering nearby. The rest of the sheep were scattered all over the countryside. That's the way things were when Sheriff Lee Mitchell reached us. His first words were, 'You were lucky those two coyotes didn't shoot you too.' Boy, was he right! The Sheriff asked if I was okay, and said he was going back to the house to call for Lonesome Pine, his deputy, and an excellent tracker. Sheriff Mitchell was intent on going after those characters. My head was throbbing! I guess I was lucky that my hat helped cushion the blow from the rock."

"Did they ever catch the two banditos?" asked Tex.

"They shore did; they're in the County jail now. Not much of a story, is it boy? I wish I had a better one than this to tell you tonight."

"It's a great story!" said Tex exuberantly. "I bet you have more too."

"He does," said Betsy, "but I think its time for young cowboys to wash up and hit the hay!"

LA FLOR, TEXAS

In 1938 La Flor, Texas was less of a town and more of a village. A visitor driving from the east to the west might have passed through it before he realized it existed. However, the town itself was nicely laid out. The central road in the town was known as Main Street. Driving into town from the east a visitor would pass First Street on his right, followed by a row of buildings also on the right side. The Post Office, Drug store, Bank, and Barber shop were all just off Main Street, while the Doctor's Office stood on the corner of Main and Crockett. If one made an immediate right onto Crockett Street, they would see the Movie House behind the Hotel and Tavern on the opposite corner, followed by the Catholic Church on the left. Opposite the Catholic Church stood the Protestant Church and cemetery. Houses where some of the more affluent townsfolk lived were just north of the churches on Bluebonnet Street. If the visitor had continued on Main Street, he would have passed the Hotel and Tavern, followed by the gas station.

On the left side of Main Street, a visitor would have noticed the Grocery Store just before Rivers General Supply and Feed Store. A left turn would put him onto Houston Street. Heading straight, one would pass the Veterinary Doctor's office on the far corner of Main and Houston, and would have seen the nearby stables and corral. Continuing down Houston Street would bring one to the railroad tracks, near which there was a small enclave of Mexicans who lived in less pretentious houses and dwellings some might call shacks. The locals often called Houston Street: "Facil", or 'Easy Street'. La Flor had a little bit of everything, the good, the ugly and the bad.

SKETCH MAP
OF
LA FLOR TEXAS

RESIDENTIAL HOMES

RESIDENTIAL HOMES

BLUEBONNET ST

CrockeTT St

First ST

CATHOLIC CHURCH

CEMETARY

PROTESTANT CHURCH

JAIL

MOVIE HOUSE

GAS STATION

HOTEL TAVERN

DOCTORS OFFICE

BANK

DRUG STORE

POST OFFICE

BARBER

MAIN ST.

VET

STABLE

RIVERS GENERAL SUPPLY AND FEED STORE

GROCERY STORE

CORRAL

RAILROAD STATION

FAIRGROUNDS

N

E

S

MEXICAN ENCLAVE

HOUSTON ST

5

Tex had heard a lot about La Flor and was anxious to see the town. The last weekend in June, the Steels made a trip to town, and Tex finally had a chance to visit Mr. Rivers' store. There, he spent a dollar of his meager funds on a new Barlow pocketknife. This purchase proved to be a great tool for helping Buckshot and meeting Tex's whittling needs. When Mr. Rivers added a new slingshot to the deal, the boy was delighted.

From there, Tex went to the drug store to purchase an ice cream cone and wait for Buckshot. It was then that he spotted the paperbacks. A rack in the store was filled to the brim with comic books and paperbacks of cowboy stories such as The Great Western, The Lone Ranger and others. The paperbacks cost twenty-five cents each, while the comic books cost a dime. The ice cream cone had only cost Tex a nickel, so he used the remainder of his funds to purchase three westerns and two comic books. He had brought two dollars into town and managed to spend it all. Now at least he would have things to do when Buckshot didn't need his help on the ranch.

Aunt Betsy had explained the loss of Zero in the November outlaw incident. This loss had upset Buckshot greatly. Zero had been a good sheepdog. He was a German Shepherd and Belgian sheepdog mix. Oscar, Buckshot's purebred Belgian sheepdog, had been doing his job alone for some seven months. Steel had been canvassing the countryside for a replacement, but with little success. Finally, near the end of June, he had read about a breeder who had some German Shepherd pups. German Shepherds were bred for jobs like handling and guarding large flocks of sheep. Their job was to act like a moving fence by constantly patrolling the flock and containing them within a given area. The German Shepherd's natural role was that of a guard and companion. They were normally gentle, but cool and aloof with strangers. Buckshot wanted a dog like this to guard his sheep. He discussed the idea with Betsy and after contacting the breeder in Texas, he expected the delivery of a puppy in July. Training the puppy would be something Tex could help him with. The puppy would be about three months old upon delivery, the perfect age to begin training. When Tex heard they were getting a puppy, he was as delighted as any boy would be.

"When will he arrive? What will his name be?" These and other excited questions came from the boy. The last question was the clincher. "Can I name him?" Tex asked. Buckshot had not anticipated such excitement from Tex. The boy needed something to love. Buckshot knew exactly what to do. He turned and nodded to Betsy, who smiled and said, "We'll give you first choice, providing you pick a name that's easy to use when calling him. The dog should arrive in Del Rio around the fourth of July, where he'll be delivered to the Rivers' house. We'll pick him up there."

This last bit of information caused Tex some concern. "That girl will see him and want him" thought the boy; "The Rivers won't let us have him. She'll probably want to name him too!" He pushed aside these thoughts and spoke out loud, "What color are shepherd dogs, Aunt Betsy?"

"They are usually black with a dusting of tan," she answered.

"Well how 'bout 'Dusty' for a name?"

"That sounds like a fine one to me." Buckshot nodded in agreement, then left the room. "We'll call the Rivers and let them know the dog will be named Dusty," said Betsy.

"Then, when you call, Aunt Betsy, will you also let them know that Kathy and Timmy can't have him?" asked Tex anxiously.

Buckshot reentered, and upon hearing Tex's last statement began to chuckle. "Don't worry son, the Rivers have no sheep and they know how badly we need another sheepdog. Dusty will be coming home with us."

July fourth, 1938 landed on a Monday. Dusty was due to be delivered on Saturday the second, and to Tex's relief he arrived on schedule. In view of the situation, the Steels decided to attend church on Sunday, then, after church, visit the carnival which had just come into town. The afternoon carnival would have to suffice for their July fourth celebration, and both adults thought Tex would greatly enjoy the festival. Jesse thought at least they ought to try the baseball toss and the BB gun duck shoot. Betsy hoped they might bump into the Rivers family so she would have a chance to chat with her sister.

The baseball toss was a success. Buckshot won a stuffed Teddy bear, and Tex won two free tickets on a merry-go-round ride. Buckshot was pleased to note how well the boy's ball throwing form had developed.

This kid might make a pitcher or a first base player on a high school baseball team one day, he thought.

Tex asked Aunt Betsy if she would like to ride on the merry-go-round with him, but she declined. She saw the Rivers walking nearby and called out, "Kathy! Tex just won two tickets for the merry-go-round. Would you like to go?"

Kathy smiled and thanked her, and to Tex's surprise she accepted the offer. The two children boarded the merry-go-round. He was dismayed that the only remaining horses on the outside row were painted white and purple. Between them was a black horse with sparkly reins mounted by a small boy of about five years. Tex knew he would have to ride the purple horse because Kathy, as the "lady" and his guest, should have the first pick. He was confident she would choose the white one, which she did. Tex had to satisfy himself that at least he could see Kathy's black hair, which was as pretty as ever, even if he only had a rear view of it.

As the merry-go-round began to move, admiring parents and friends waved and cheered the riders from behind a low fence around the perimeter. The young boy sitting in front of Tex began waving his arms, jumping up and down, and generally showing off. The merry-go-round was turning at top speed when the lad tried to stand up in his saddle. Seeing this, the operator panicked and slammed on the machine's brakes, causing the merry-go-round to lurch and the young boy to go flying off his horse. Tex yelled and moved like a flash, grabbing the boy's arm just as he hit the rim of the machine's base. There were screams in the crowd and a man leaped over the fence, racing to help Tex and the young boy. Tex was holding the youngster's arm with one hand and a merry-go-round pole with the other. He looked up, a mixture of annoyance and bravery on his face, "You know this kid?" he asked. "He's my son," the man replied.

The boy was bawling to beat the band but except for some scratches he was unhurt. The father lifted the boy and returned him to his mother. He walked back and shook Tex's hand saying, "Thank you son, for your quick action. Mikey might have been hurt worse if you hadn't grabbed him."

"You're welcome, sir. It wasn't any big deal," said Tex politely. He turned and saw Kathy's face which much to his surprise was ashen and she didn't say a word. Tex turned and walked back to join the Steels. Buckshot and Betsy each gave him a hug, saying how proud they were. He would have preferred to hear Kathy saying those things and being hugged by her. But he didn't save the boy to impress her. He did it to help the kid and that was that. Besides, now they were going to go get the new puppy.

The Rivers returned before the Steels arrived. They had the pup, plus a bag of puppy food and some written instructions for his care, ready when the Steels appeared.

Kathy was standing near her father when Jim Rivers handed the pup to Jesse and Tex, a few steps behind the Steels. Kathy left her father's side and walked towards him. She smiled and said in a soft voice, "Tex, what you did on the merry-go-round today was so brave. Everybody was impressed. I know you will have fun with the puppy. You ought to call him 'Dusty', he's so dirty from playing in the yard."

"Why that's the name we've already picked, thanks!"

On the way home Betsy outlined some of her rules for the pup. "First, Dusty will not be a house dog. Second, he will not take priority over chores. Third, he will *not* be a house dog."

"Ma'am, you already said the third rule first." Tex replied.

"So I did, so I did." she answered with a chuckle.

"Aunt Betsy, can we build a dog house just outside my window so I can see Dusty? I don't want no coyotes getting him."

"Don't say 'no coyotes'" she corrected him, "say 'any coyotes'. And Jesse will have to okay the dog house location."

"Yes ma'am!"

Jesse spoke up, "Tex, we can build a doghouse outside your window. That'll give Dusty and Snickers a chance to become friends. Then after a little while, when Dusty is a mite bigger, we'll bring a couple of sheep down and pen them nearby so he can begin to get some idea about his future job. That pup's going to have to learn fast because I need him up there helping Oscar this winter."

The ride home from the Rivers' house was the happiest Jesse and Betsy had known for a long time. There was a continuing stream of giggles and laughter coming from the back seat. The boy had the puppy in his arms and was thoroughly enjoying the furry little creature. The pup seemed to take to the boy, covering his face with wet puppy kisses. It was a happy day they would remember for a long time.

6

The last time anyone in La Flor had seen rain was the day after Tex arrived at the Steel's ranch. June was hot and July hotter, with the temperature often reaching one hundred or more degrees. The sheep had moved off the ridge and were now foraging at lower brushy elevations along the creek, whose flow had been reduced to a trickle. The cattle suffered as well, congregating in what shade they could find from the mesquite trees and small Texas scrub-oaks and gathering water from the two windmill sites. Telephone conversations between neighboring ranchers became more and more gloomy. In a matter of days, a decision would be made to start up the butane tanks and burners in order to burn the thorns off the cactus. This effort would insure the cattle could have something to eat. Jesse explained to Tex that when the S-> ranch began the burning process, Betsy's job would be to bring water to the thirsty workers. Tex should help as directed.

The cactus burning began on a neighboring ranch west of the S-> ranch. Buckshot was planning to go help his neighbor the next morning and leave Tex at the ranch to take care of the chores. Around mid-afternoon, Betsy went down to the gate to pick up the mail and found a small envelope among the letters addressed to Tex. When her two 'men' came in that evening for supper she handed the envelope to Tex.

"Look, I think it's from Kathy," she said smiling.

Indeed it was. It contained an invitation to Kathy's birthday party and picnic on Saturday, August 6th, at three o'clock in the afternoon.

"Wow," said Tex obviously pleased. "Aunt Betsy, what do you do at a birthday party? I've never been to one before."

Betsy was astounded, "You mean to tell me your father and stepmother have never even given you a party?"

"No ma'am."

Betsy looked thoughtful, "Well, at a birthday party you go and have fun, eat hot dogs, cake and ice cream, and you take a gift."

"What kind of gift?" the boy asked "I don't have much money left; I think I'm down to about five dollars now."

"You don't have to buy her a gift," said Betsy "you can make one."

The remainder of supper was spent discussing the forthcoming birthday party. In the course of the conversation Betsy asked Tex when his birthday was.

"September 11th, I think," he answered.

"Well, how about that, mine's September 12th," Buckshot interjected. "And by the way, I've an idea for a nice birthday gift for Kathy. It's one we can make out of the shell of an armadillo's back."

"But we don't have any shells!" said Tex.

"We will if you go hunt one down. I saw an armadillo out by the south end of the creek just the other day. You can take the 20 gauge shotgun and go get him."

The next morning after breakfast Tex questioned Betsy. He had some misgivings about the armadillo hunt.

"If I shoot the armadillo, what would we make from the shell on its back? What about my chores? Who is going to do them while I'm out hunting?"

"Why you could make a hair barrette," she answered "The lower part of the back has a nice bend that can be pinned over a girl's ponytail by inserting a pretty stick through two holes in the shell." Betsy demonstrated with her own hair barrette which she retrieved from her bedroom.

"I'm just not sure I'll find one and that we'll have enough time for it to be ready. The birthday party is only a little over a week away."

"Why don't you give it a try?" she suggested. "It's a nice morning and you don't have to be gone all day. You can do your chores after you return from hunting."

Not long after this conversation, Tex began walking slowly towards the creek bed with the shotgun and several 20 gauge shells in his pocket. At his slow hunter's pace, he would arrive at the creek in about thirty minutes. He had not gone too far, when he felt a presence behind him. A funny brownish creature was coming down the trail.

"It looks like Dusty." Tex said to himself. Somehow the pup had found a hole in his pen fencing and had followed his new master down the path. "Dusty, what are you doing here?" Tex stooped and grinned at the dog,

"You don't know anything about armadillos." He stood up, "OK, you can come with me, you bad, happy pup!"

When they reached the creek bed Tex and Dusty poked around searching mostly through the brush alongside the creek. No armadillos came busting out of the brush. After searching for some time, Tex decided to sit down and cool off for a spell and the pup lay beside him. It was very peaceful and pleasant beside the water, thought Tex. It was only a matter of minutes before the tired boy and dog dozed off. He awoke suddenly when the pup lying on his lap made a sudden move to get up. A rabbit was hopping down the trail and paused, but spotting the boy and dog began to quickly move away. The pup bolted after the rabbit and the chase was on. Tex jumped up and began running after Dusty, leaving the shotgun on the ground. He saw the pup turn and dash into the center of some heavy brush. Then all was quiet.

"Where did Dusty go?" thought Tex.

He walked around and around the vicinity of the brush, but couldn't see or hear a sound. He moved to his hands and knees and began to crawl towards the center of the thick brush. Suddenly, he saw a flash of metal. It was the dog tag attached to Dusty's collar. A stick had wedged itself under his collar and pinned the dog to a branch. The pup wasn't hurt but was sitting and panting happily, waiting for his master to come and find him. Dusty's fur was a mess and full of brambles. Tex was scratched up on his legs, arms, face and hands. He retrieved the young dog and crawled back out of the bushes. Still holding Dusty, Tex walked back to his spot by the creek and picked up the shotgun. Boy and dog walked back to the ranch house.

Betsy had been on the lookout for the boy's return. It was about lunchtime when she spotted Tex and Dusty approaching the house. Tex put Dusty back in his enclosure and plugged the escape hole with a board. When he entered the house Betsy exclaimed, "My, what did you get into? You're a mess." Tex grinned and told Betsy of his adventure.

"There's a lot of ticks, chiggers, and poison ivy down there now," said Betsy creasing her forehead almost into a frown. "I want you to shed those clothes and get into the tub to wash off." She handed Tex a bar of thick, strong smelling soap. "Here's some soap—get to work!"

Tex did as he was told. After lunch he began to itch all over his body. He scratched his face, arms and legs. By suppertime small blisters appeared on his arms, legs and even his face. At supper the scratching continued.

Jesse and Betsy noticed this and suspected that he had crawled into a stand of poison oak or poison ivy—or both.

"Do we have any calamine lotion in the house?" Buckshot asked, looking at Tex across the supper table.

"A little," replied Betsy "I keep it only in case I get the stuff—since you're not allergic to either weed."

That night Tex hardly slept, thanks to the itching caused by the blisters now appearing all over his body. The electric fan Betsy had placed in the room provided little relief from the hot summer night. Finally he fell asleep.

When Buckshot walked into Tex's room the following morning, he could hardly believe what he saw. Tex's face was swollen and one eye was sealed shut. Poison oak blisters covered his arms, legs and face. The boy wouldn't be going anywhere for a while.

After speaking with the Doctor over the telephone, Buckshot and Betsy began the prescribed treatment of Epsom salt baths two or three times a day, followed by a liberal application of calamine lotion. The kid was in total misery, his only comfort being the promise that the ailment should last about ten days.

"Aunt Betsy," called Tex from his bedroom, after he had begun feeling slightly better, "I think I won't be going to the birthday party, not with all this poison oak."

"I'll let Ruth know, Tex," answered Betsy. "I'm going to La Flor now to pick up more medical supplies for you. I'll be back soon!"

"Poor kid," she thought as she drove to town. "With all those scabs and sores and not knowing any of Kathy's friends, I don't blame him for not wanting to go. We'll just have to do something for his birthday in September. Every child should have a celebration on his or her birthday." Suddenly, she remembered that Jesse's birthday was the day after Tex's. "Maybe we could combine the two events!" she thought as the car kicked up dust behind her on the road to town.

$$7$$

The problems with the August heat continued. Ranchers and even La Flor folk got up at daybreak and worked until midday. Midday until about four in the afternoon was reserved for "siesta" time. Work resumed until sunset, followed by a hearty supper, reading or listening to the news via the radio. Bedtime was early and needed. One particular August evening found Buckshot and the boy sitting quietly on the front porch, listening to the crickets sing in spite of the hot summer air.

"You're mighty quiet, boy," said Buckshot. "Thinking about anything special?" "Yes sir," replied Tex. "I was thinking about the cowboy story I just read, about a bank robbery. Have there ever been any bank robberies in La Flor?"

"Well come to think of it, there was one attempt," said Jesse with a chuckle. "You know that fellow that cleans the streets and sort of picks up around town? The one everybody calls Fuzzy? Well, his real name is Will Tinker. He's kind of a parolee at the jail, does odd jobs for Sheriff Mitchell and sleeps in one of the cells at night. Everybody in town knows him, and knows he doesn't have all four cylinders working. I guess that's why he got the nickname 'Fuzzy'. Fuzzy Tinker, get it? Well, one day he tried to rob the bank." Jesse continued. "He somehow got his poor old mother to let him drive her old Model T Ford into town. He parked in front of the bank leaving the motor running while he ran inside waving a pistol around. We found out later it wasn't loaded, but that didn't stop him from running around yelling 'This is a stick-up! This is a stick-up!' The teller working the counter looked at him pretty calmly and asked, 'What are you trying to do Fuzzy, scare us all to death?' Startled by this, Fuzzy reached up and touched his face with his free hand and yelled, 'Oh dagnabit! I forgot to put on my mask!'

Fuzzy ran outside to his car, got the mask, put it on, and then ran back to the front door of the bank. However the teller had wisely locked the door before Fuzzy returned. Fuzzy was still pounding on the door yelling 'Let me in! Let me in!' when Sheriff Mitchell came and took him away."

By this time both Buckshot and Tex were laughing hard enough to beat all get out. "I don't remember exactly what sentence Judge Henry Bryan gave him, but poor old Fuzzy has no real home, and most folks hereabout won't hire him for anything. Sheriff Mitchell has worked out something where Fuzzy sleeps at the jail and does chores around town. He gets what you might call room and board, and a very small cash allowance. It seems to be working well; it helps the town and helps Fuzzy. Maybe one day that fourth cylinder will kick in, but I wouldn't hold my breath waiting until it does."

The boy continued laughing as Betsy appeared at the door. "Tex, I'd like you to come in now so we can go over some grammar words I gave you and you can practice your handwriting. Jesse keeps you so busy helping him train Dusty and with other chores that your schooling is being neglected."

"Schooling is one thing," thought Tex, "among others that I don't miss." Tex hoped that the next time Buckshot told a story it would be about his time as a Marine in the World War.

Betsy understood the importance and need for laughter and joy in their lives, especially during those hot August days. So at least one evening during the week, usually Fridays, she kept reserved for music and singing. It had been a particularly hot Friday, when both of her 'men' returned to the house around suppertime. They were tired and soaked with perspiration. After they showered and had eaten, Betsy announced "Tonight is music night. I'm going to get my guitar and play some tunes for you men." At this, Jesse said "Wonderful! I'll go get my harmonica and help. And Tex, how about accompanying us with this washboard and spoon? I'll show you how easy it will be." It didn't take long for three smiling faces to combine their musical efforts successfully—and the mini-hoe down began, with Betsy leading the group.

They played and sang songs like "Over There", "My Bonnie Lies Over the Ocean", "Yellow Rose of Texas" and cowboy tunes like "Git Along Little Doggie". When Betsy and Jesse broke into the hillbilly song, "Three Shiftless Skunks", Tex started laughing so hard tears ran down his face. Even the dog Snickers joined in with some lusty howling. "Teach me the song, teach me the song!" Tex pleaded happily.

"OK, here's how it goes." Buckshot sang,

> *"Three shiftless skunks are we*
> *From the hills of Tennessee*
> *And we don't put on no bodacious airs*
> *But our beards are often seen*
> *In the Esquire Magazine*
> *Showing what the well dressed*
> *Hillbilly wears!"*

The evening ended with "The Saints Go Marching In" with Betsy leading her happy men into the sitting room. "Whew, that was great, Aunt Betsy and Buckshot. I'm tuckered out and I'm ready for bed. Goodnight!"

"Goodnight Tex!" they both responded, "Sleep well!"

The scorching days of August ended with a good two-day rain shower that lasted until midday on September first, ending all cactus burning. The following Monday was Labor Day. However most of the holiday activities took place on Saturday. Even so, this Labor Day Saturday was not much different to Tex than most Saturdays he had spent with the Steels.

Labor Day was a day the ranchers, their wives, and young ones came to town to purchase supplies and socialize a bit. Doc Hammerstein's drug store was busy serving ice cream and soda pop to the children who sat on stools at the counter. Some adults sat at the small round tables drinking coffee, smoking, and making light chitchat. The rain had put everyone in a good mood. Even the grass was showing signs of life with a touch of pale green on its blades.

Ruth Rivers and Betsy Steel were seated in a far corner at a table and appeared to be engaged in animated conversation.

"Betsy, I'm so glad you came to town today. It seems like forever since I've seen you!" Ruth exclaimed.

"Well, I'm glad to see you too. I wanted to pick your brains and see what you think of an idea."

"What idea?"

"A joint birthday party for Jesse and little Tex. They have back to back birthdays. Jesse's is the twelfth and the boy's is Sunday, the day before, on the eleventh. Tex will be fourteen and Jesse will be thirty-eight, I think. He never talks about his age much. I know he enlisted in the Marines after he turned seventeen and arrived in France in the late summer of

1918. Jesse participated in some of the fiercest fighting and was wounded. We haven't done much about birthdays over the years. I don't think the boy has ever had a birthday party, and I thought we could combine their celebrations on Sunday the eleventh, after the church service. What do you think, Ruth?"

"Betsy, I think it's a fine idea." Ruth looked excited at the prospect of the party. They discussed the details for the celebration, parting in happy anticipation of the joint birthday party.

The early days of September passed quickly. Sunday morning, the eleventh of September, found Betsy up bright and early.

"Rise and shine, you sleepy heads!" she called out. "It's time you were up and dressed for church. It's going to be a beautiful day!"

Buckshot and Tex walked sleepily into the kitchen, tucking in their shirt tails and rubbing their eyes.

"Sit down, sit down." Betsy fussed happily around the room. "The early bird gets the worm!" Jesse smiled but Tex in his early morning stupor looked puzzled. He hadn't seen Aunt Betsy this happy in a while.

The service began at eleven, and since Buckshot always wanted to be on time, he hurried his lady and the boy into the car by ten. The trio was passing through a remote area of the wide-open Texas ranch landscape about halfway to town, when suddenly, bad luck struck. Pow! The right tire blew, leaving them stuck and requiring some fast action to change the tire. Jesse reacted with speed after expressing a hearty, "Damn! We didn't need this, Lord!" He methodically began sorting out the equipment needed to change the flat. "Tex, I could sure use some help."

Man and boy worked hard and efficiently, but both were perspiring and looked a little ruffled as they jumped back into the car. Try as Buckshot might, the car would only go so fast. They finally arrived in town about twenty minutes after the service had started. The Reverend Joshua Creedon was well into his sermon.

"We all have gifts that differ according to the grace given to us. Use them wisely and remember the Lord *giveth,* and the Lord *taketh* away." His voice boomed emphatically throughout the little chapel in heavy Texas drawl as the Steels and Tex crept into the rear-most seats. Once seated all three assumed rapt expressions of attentiveness in hopes of drawing minimum attention to their late arrival.

The service continued smoothly with the Reverend exhorting the congregation to serve the Lord and do good deeds. At the end, Reverend Creedon invited everyone into the meeting hall for a "most gloriously *special* event." It took a while for the congregation to assemble and the children to place themselves in full view of the "ceremony".

Reverend Creedon announced "*Ladies* and *gentlemen*. Today is a *very* special day for two *very* special people in this *highly* esteemed *congregation*." He dramatically emphasized the last half of 'congregation'. "Young Jake Hall here, known to you all as *Tex,* and our *good friend* Jesse Steel, are *celebrating* in this *good* company, their birthdays today and tomorrow, *respectively*." He turned with a dramatic pause to face the wide eyed youngsters in the front row. He continued, "Today is Tex's *fourteenth* birthday and tomorrow will be Jesse's *eighty-third*." The congregation erupted in laughter. "Or did I *reverse* the numbers Jesse? Anyway, let's *all* sing Happy Birthday to the both of them."

The crowd sang with exuberance as Tex and Buckshot stood smiling and looking slightly embarrassed.

When they finished, Jesse spoke, "Thank you Pastor and Tex. I thank all of you for being here with us today. It's a happy day for me and Betsy to be able to share this celebration with young Tex here.

As you may recall, he was fairly new to our ranch when we went to town on the third of July to pick up our new pup. After church that day we decided to see what was happening at the carnival. It was there, during a merry-go-round ride, that a young boy fell off his horse while the machine was still turning and only the quick action of young Tex here saved the boy from serious injury. When a young cowpoke does a thing like that, I'd say he has earned his spurs, don't you agree?" The congregation applauded enthusiastically as Jesse, Betsy, and the Rivers family came forward with a beautifully wrapped box.

"Tex, this is for you. Happy Birthday!" Jesse exclaimed.

When Tex opened the box, his happy excitement brought smiles and more applause from the assembled group. The box contained a beautiful pair of working spurs, just like those the Texas cowboys used. The kid was thrilled.

"Can I try them on now?" he asked.

"You sure can smiled Buckshot, "but be careful when you go down the stairs! You'll need to turn your feet sideways so you won't trip."

Betsy and the group presented Jesse with a new lariat which he said was, "just what he needed!" Kathy and Ruth began cutting the two birthday cakes. The pastor said the blessing, "Thank you Lord for the honor bestowed upon this young cowboy, for this *bounty*, these *birthdays* and these *good* people." And everyone said "Amen!"

The children gathered around Tex to look at his new spurs, while the elders congregated around the Steels and the Rivers. Kathy even came over to wish Tex a very happy birthday. It was a celebration to remember!

Jesse, Betsy and Tex were all smiles as they headed home. There wasn't much talking; each was deep in his or her own thoughts. Finally, Buckshot broke the silence. "Tex, we don't want to spoil your day, but I think you should know that yesterday we got a phone call from Arizona. Betsy answered the phone. Why don't you tell him what happened?"

"The call surprised me. I didn't realize at first who was calling, but it was your stepmother," said Betsy. "Your father has become very ill and they've taken him to Arizona to recover. He's in a sanitarium, which is sort of a hospital. She didn't go into details about his illness, but she said they expected it would take about four or five months for him to recover. They asked us to keep you here through Christmas, and we agreed to do so. We hope that's okay by you."

"Okay?" Tex looked up, "Thank you. That's about the best news you could have given me! I hope I will be able to stay with you always."

"Well," Buckshot looked thoughtful "you're welcome to stay, but now that you've earned your spurs you're going to have to do a little more to earn your keep. I have a new enterprise in mind where you and I can be partners and earn some cash. We can talk about it tomorrow."

"Can you give me a hint?" Tex asked anxiously.

"In October it will be the time of year when we can begin trapping animals like foxes, raccoons, and ringtail cats. We can market their hides; there's a great demand for furs these days. I think we can earn enough for you to have some spending money and enough for Aunt Betsy and me, to help pay for your room and board. I have about four traps you can use to get started on. I'll show you how they work, and if it looks like we'll need more we can always get them later. With a dozen or so traps we should be able to make near sixty dollars a month. We'll split the proceeds fifty-fifty. How does that sound?"

"When do I start?" asked Tex in his most business-like voice.

"We can start tomorrow afternoon," said Buckshot with a chuckle, "after you finish your chores and working with Dusty. I haven't checked on him for a couple of weeks now. How's Dusty doing?"

"He's doing fine, Buckshot. He's doing just fine!" He turned to Aunt Betsy. "When we get home, can I bring Dusty into the kitchen and show Buckshot what he can do?"

"Why don't you bring Dusty up on the front porch? You can show Jesse what he can do there." The minute they arrived home, Tex went in search of Dusty, returning proudly to the porch to demonstrate to Buckshot all he had taught his pup.

"Dusty, sit!" The pup sat. "Dusty, shake hands! Shake!" Dusty raised his paw and placed it in Buckshot's hand.

Tex smiled, "That's what I taught him, isn't he great?"

"That's fine, son. Tomorrow, let's see what he can do with the sheep."

"Jesse," Betsy appeared at the door, "don't expect too much. After all Dusty is only about six months old, if that."

"Oh, and there's one more thing," the excited boy exclaimed as Tex ran to his room. When he returned he held a paper bag containing a mysterious object.

"Buckshot, I know it's not your birthday until tomorrow, but here's your present. I made it myself."

Buckshot took the bag and extracted the gift. It was a cigar box with a rectangular hole cut in the top. The opening was covered with a piece of window screen.

"Do you like it?" the boy asked anxiously. Jesse didn't say anything, mostly because he wasn't quite sure what it was. Thankfully, Tex didn't wait for his reply.

"It's a music box, a cricket music box I made for you. I'll go catch some crickets and put them in it so you can hear them sing this evening."

That evening on the front porch, Buckshot put the cricket box to his ear and listened as they began to sing.

"Thanks Tex," he said, "this has been my best birthday in a long time."

"This was my best birthday ever!"

8

Just then, the telephone began ringing. Buckshot left the porch quickly to answer the call. It was Sheriff Lee Mitchell.

"Jesse, will you be coming to town tomorrow or Tuesday?"

"Hadn't planned on coming in tomorrow. We just returned from church and we're chock-a-block with things to do around the ranch, especially tomorrow! Why do you ask?"

"Well," the Sheriff answered, "Judge O'Brien called me and a couple of pretty big things for La Flor have come up. First, Enrique Herrero, the long time and famous peace officer from the El Paso area is coming to visit us. You may recall, he's about the most prominent Mexican law officer we've had in these parts for many years, and I wanted you to meet him. He's a fairly old man now and retired, but Herrero commands a lot of respect. He was instrumental in getting El Paso incorporated as a town, enabling the citizens there to elect their own mayor and other city officials. Judge O'Brien wants some of us to chat with Enrique about us becoming designated as a town. The judge thinks La Flor is ready for this, and we want to get our best citizens in this area involved."

"Thanks, Lee," responded Buckshot, "When is everyone going to meet with Señor Herrero?"

"Actually, I don't think it will happen until Wednesday or Thursday."

"Wednesday or Thursday would work better for me. Please give me a call when you have a better handle on the time frame, and I'll make every effort to be there."

"Thanks, Jesse, I'll call you as soon as I know the firm details."

"Wouldn't you know," mused Buckshot, "The Lord must have some reason for this! So, Tex, we'll have to wait awhile to get our trapping business started. October will be a better month for trapping anyway, and we can use the time in between now and then to start on the other thing I had on my mind."

"What's the other thing?" Tex asked.

"Learning to drive the Ford tractor," Buckshot answered, turning his head towards his wife.

"Betsy, I hope you don't have any objections to this, but Tex is fourteen now and I need help getting feed and other things up to the cattle. Tex could be of more help to me if he could drive the tractor once in a while."

"I agree Jesse," responded Betsy, and turning to Tex she inquired, "How does becoming an S-arrow ranch tractor driver sound to you?"

"Wow!" exclaimed Tex, "It sounds great. When do we start, Buckshot?"

"This week!" answered Buckshot. "I don't think I'll be getting too involved with Judge O'Brien's and Lee Mitchell's political goings-on, but I do think it would pay for me to know what they are up to, so I will attend that meeting, when Lee gets me the information."

The meeting in La Flor was postponed until the following week, so the tractor driving lessons began promptly, much to Tex's delight. As they walked to the tractor that Monday morning, Buckshot began the teaching session.

"Tex, this tractor has all the same gears and mechanisms as our Ford automobile. It just doesn't go as fast."

With the boy seated in the vehicle, Buckshot went over each of the important features including the on-off switch, gears, brakes and lights. He then seated himself behind the boy and started the engine. Putting the vehicle into low gear and easing up on the clutch moved the tractor slowly forward. Buckshot then showed Tex how to put the tractor into the other gears, including reverse and stopping.

"Now it's your turn, Tex," he said. As was expected, the boy made some mistakes, but proved himself to be an eager and attentive student. The first lesson lasted almost an hour. When they finished, Buckshot complimented Tex, then sent him off to do some of his customary chores.

By the end of the week, Tex had improved enough so Buckshot was able to walk alongside the moving tractor and coach the boy while he drove around a field. That evening, during supper, the main topic of conversation was "tractor driving." Smiling as he looked at his wife, Buckshot commented, "Betsy, I believe Tex can take the tractor out on his own next week. Hopefully this will prove helpful to you while I'm in town, meeting with the Judge Lee, our important visitor, and others they may have assembled. If there's a problem you can call Jim Rivers at the store and I'm sure whoever answers can track me down. Jim will probably be at the meeting too!"

On Tuesday, the following week, Buckshot drove to town. Arrangements had been made with Ruth for Buckshot to spend the night at the Rivers' house, since the big meeting was expected to begin early and last all day on Wednesday.

Tex was up and about early Wednesday morning. After breakfast he went outside and began tackling his assigned chores. Around mid-morning he returned to the house for a glass of milk and a snack, and found Aunt Betsy bustling about.

"Tex," she said, "I've just received a call from Otto Schultz, one of our neighbors, whose ranch borders our property on the northeast side. Mrs. Shultz is very ill and Otto's car won't start. He asked me to come over and help take her to the hospital in Del Rio. I'm leaving now and probably won't be back until late this afternoon. I want you to go to the north field and drop off that load of hay Buckshot put on the trailer. You can pull it out there with the tractor. Be careful."

"You be careful, Aunt Betsy, and don't worry about me," replied Tex, "I'll be fine!"

After Betsy had departed, Tex walked out of the house and was greeted by Snickers and Dusty. "You guys," he said, "better take notice. I'm the boss here now and you'll have to do everything I say." Both dogs wagged their tails as he patted each dog on the back. "Now I better get that hay moved to the north field."

Since the trailer was already hitched to the tractor, Tex believed his task could be completed quickly. As soon as the hay was unloaded he drove back to the barn and unhitched the trailer. It had been pretty windy the previous night, but the day was now calm and beautiful. The outlook for the afternoon appeared to be uneventful, slow and boring.

"So," he said to himself, "I think I'll saddle Star up and take her for a ride. With all that wind last night, it might be a good idea to check the fence line for breaks." After saddling Star, he led her over to the gate to the north field. Once through the gate, and after closing it, Tex mounted the pony. As he rode along the fence line, he heard a cow bawling. Something was wrong. This was a distress bawl, and it was coming from the gully on the far side of the very large pasture.

When he arrived at the edge of the gully, two coyotes ran from the top of the opposite side. They ran about 100 yards then stopped, as if to watch and see what was going to happen next. Their dinner was lying pinned between the branches of a dead tree which had likely been blown down by the wind during the night. A cow was standing in the gully nearby. Her calf was pinned beneath the blow down and she was not going to let those coyotes harm her calf if she could help it.

Tex immediately sized up this most unusual problem. To free the calf, who may or may not be badly injured, he had to move the tree. This could be done by tying a rope around the upper part of the tree and pulling the tree with the tractor at least enough to free the calf. The cow wasn't going to let the coyotes get near the calf and probably would not let Tex near it either. How was he going to distract the cow long enough to slide down into the gully, secure one end of the rope to the tree, get out of the ditch without being gored by the cow, and then tie the other end to the tractor trailer hitch?

He decided to return to the barn to retrieve the tractor and the length of rope he needed, as well as three lariats from saddles inside the barn. If necessary, the lariats would be tied end to end to make the rope long enough for the job. As he was doing these things, he heard Dusty and Snickers barking furiously from inside the fenced yard around the house.

Tex looked at the dogs and yelled, "Hush dogs!" Then he got an idea. What if he took Snickers along and tied him to the back of the tractor? Snickers would not like being tied up and would surely begin barking. The cow, thinking another coyote was on the scene, would go after Snickers, who could hide behind the large tractor wheel. While the cow was distracted by Snickers, Tex would slide down the hill, tie the rope around the tree and climb back up to the tractor.

Feeling confident this plan would work, Tex captured Snickers and attached a leash to his collar. Then holding the little dog in his arm, he drove the tractor back to the area of the blow down.

The coyotes had returned and the cow was down in the gully where she could defend her calf. Tex parked the tractor and tied Snickers with the leash to the tractor's trailer hitch. Snickers began barking as Tex walked away from the tractor. The cow scrambled up the hill to confront her new enemy. Tex slid down the hillside to the bottom of the gully, ran to the tree and tied one end of the line to it. The coyotes again retreated.

Seeing Tex at the tree, the cow turned and went down the gully to protect her calf. Tex climbed up the opposite bank, barely escaping the wrath of the cow. When he reached the top of the gully, he realized he was on the opposite side from the tractor. This problem was solved by walking along the top of the gully until he came to a bend where he could slide down and climb up the tractor side of the gully. To insure the cow wouldn't see him, Tex wisely made a wide looping return and reached the tractor without incident. There he took up as much slack in the line that he could and secured this end to the tractor hitch. With Snickers again in his arms, he climbed aboard the tractor and started the engine. With the tractor in low gear, Tex eased up on the clutch and the vehicle began to move, pulling the tree enough to allow the calf to free himself.

After backing the tractor a few feet, Tex untied the line, and proceeded to return to the barn with Snickers. The calf rescue had taken most of the afternoon. As Tex reached the barn with the tractor, Buckshot returned from town and parked his car near the barn. Seeing the boy on the tractor he immediately inquired, "Tex, what's been going on? How come you're on the tractor with Snickers? Where's the Mrs.?"

Tex climbed down from the tractor and released a very happy Snickers. He breathlessly related the story of the calf rescue to Buckshot. When Buckshot asked about the calf, he replied, "I don't know if the calf is injured. I was going to go back up there on Star and see if I could get closer to the calf and see if he's hurt."

"Tell you what, son," Buckshot said, "Let's both go back up there and check that calf out. You lead the way on Star, and I'll follow on the tractor. When we get up there, we'll bring the cow with her calf back to the barn where I can inspect both of them more easily." Upon returning to the barn, Buckshot told Tex how pleased he was. He then added, "Tex, wait until Aunt Betsy hears about this. She's going to be real impressed and I expect she'll be as proud of you as I am. The cow and calf will stay penned up for a few days until I'm sure the cuts and scratches he received will heal without any infections. Thank you very much for handling this situation so well." With this, he put his arm around the boy as they walked to the house.

That evening the stars in the sky could not hold a candle to the sparkle in Tex's eyes.

9

The 1930's were years of hard times in the United States. By 1938 in some areas, unemployment was as high as twenty percent. Many folks in rural areas not only hunted, but trapped in order to provide meat for the table and extra income from selling the skins. Fox, raccoon and even skunk furs were in high demand, as Jesse Steel well knew.

Europe was also in a time of turmoil. General Francisco Franco's rebellion in Spain had garnered significant U.S. opposition. In fact, a brigade of soldiers called the Lincoln Brigade was being organized in New York City. Many of its recruits were unemployed men seeking steady income. The brigade ultimately recruited more than a thousand men for service in Spain.

As for the Steels, their survival and that of the S-> Arrow ranch was the most important thing on their minds. They had lost a son, but God in His wisdom had blessed them with Tex, a willing lad who was helping to "hold the other end" for a limited period of time, at least through the Christmas holiday.

On Saturday morning, October 1st, before they went to town, Tex Hall received indoctrination into the realm of trapping. Buckshot, ever the teacher, explained the history of trapping to Tex, the reasons for it, and the proper way to proceed. He showed Tex his four leg hold traps. He demonstrated the proper way to prepare the site with a small horseshoe-like hole to place the trap in, and then how to build a 'vee' shaped fence out of sticks. The fence would channel the animal to bait placed behind the trap, on the ground inside the apex of the fence. Having explained and demonstrated the trapping process, Buckshot and his young student headed out to put into action what had been taught. Betsy provided some table scraps of meat they could use for bait.

Off they went, down the same trail Tex and Dusty had taken on their unfortunate armadillo excursion. When they reached the creek bed, Buckshot made a sharp left turn and began preparing the first trap site.

"You can tell a lot of game have used this trail from those tracks in the dirt. The animals find water as well as food in this location." Buckshot walked about another fifty yards or so and set in the second trap. "OK Tex, it's your turn now. The next two traps are for you to put in place." Buckshot continued his explanation "What we are doing is kind of like what Marines did in France. When we went out on a patrol in no-man's land we, that is my squad and I, never came back to friendly lines the same way we went out. We'll use this method after setting our traps. This way we don't overly contaminate the air and the ground with our scent. Animals have very good noses and they can know a human has been around long after he has left the area.

"The next important thing is to remember where all your traps were set." Buckshot now looked Tex in the eye, "Dusty is never to go with you when you are walking along our trap line tomorrow or any other day. It is ethical and proper to walk the trap lines daily and not less than every other day. When you are not able to walk the lines, I will.

You should take the 20 gauge shotgun with you for protection, but don't shoot any animals caught in the traps. Get a good stick and knock them in the head, so as not to damage the fur. That's the tough part, we want to put them down quickly and humanely. You're big enough and strong enough to do this, but I'll go with you the first time or two to ensure you learn all the right things to do. Any skinning will be done up at the barn, I'll teach you how to do that when the time comes."

Tex proved to be a good student and quickly became an effective trapper. Most days when he walked the trap line he would return home with a couple of gray foxes and raccoons or ringtail cats. It was only a short time before Buckshot increased the trap line to twelve traps.

One bright sunny October morning greeted young Tex, and became the trapping day neither he nor the Steels would ever forget. He left the house in the early hours of light and harvested a gray fox from the first trap. As he approached the 10th trap he knew what to expect before he arrived. A skunk had been caught and in his anger had soaked the area with his scent.

Tex knew that shooting the skunk was against the rules Buckshot had established. But how was he to get close enough so he could zap the animal with his stick, and not get zapped himself? There just wasn't a good way. Finally, to eliminate him, he laid the fox on the ground and dashed in as fast as he could to make the kill. Although Tex nailed the skunk, the skunk zapped Tex first. His clothes were drenched with Skunk urine. The smell was so bad he could hardly breathe. He put a bandanna over his nose and carefully extracted the skunk from the trap. Picking up the fox with his other hand, he walked back towards the ranch house.

Aunt Betsy was in the yard hanging the wash on her clothesline. She didn't see Tex as he approached, but she sure smelled him and immediately knew what had happened.

"J-e-s-s-e," she screamed "Get over here pronto! Our boy has been gotten by a skunk!"

Jesse came running and as soon as he saw and smelled Tex he yelled out, "Stop! Don't come any closer to the house until we say so!"

Betsy had already started filling the half fifty-five gallon drum which was sitting on concrete blocks. Jesse began building a fire under the tub. A large jug of tomato juice was poured into the tub and for good measure, Betsy threw in a bar of homemade brown lye soap.

"I'm ready for him now" Betsy called to Jesse. "Put these towels where he can reach them and tell him to take off all his clothes, then come up here and get in this tub. And Jesse, that water is hot enough now, so put out that fire!"

Buckshot suppressed his laughter, but neither he nor Betsy wanted to be tainted by the skunk smell. He called out to Tex, "Son, take off all your clothes—everything! It is now bath time! You can wear your boots up here and bring the shotgun, but nothing else!"

"I can't do that!" the miserable boy cried. "I'm not coming buck naked as long as Aunt Betsy is in the yard!"

"Betsy," Jesse laughed, "I think you should go into the house now. I'll handle this from here on. We'll need some clean clothes though. Hopefully we can get him pretty well cleaned up."

With Betsy in the house Tex came walking in slowly and very ashamed. He sat in the tub for what seemed like hours, scrubbing and scrubbing to get rid of the smell. Most of the smell came off but not entirely. The Steels decided it was bearable and hoped the smell would disappear in a few days, which it did.

Later on, when they could chuckle about the incident, Buckshot informed Tex, "Son, I'm modifying one of the trapping rules I gave you. If we catch another skunk in the trap—get as far away as you can and shoot him. We'll let some of the hungry foxes and raccoons take care of him, if they are that hungry."

"Yes sir!" Tex said with a laugh.

With the onset of the fall season, Buckshot, even with Tex's help, had almost more to do than he could handle. Tex's days were busy. He continued to check on the sheep at least every other day as well as walk his trap line, which became more fruitful as Tex improved in his ability to set the traps in good locations and rig them effectively. The first big check totaled sixty dollars, which Buckshot split evenly with Tex.

When they went to town the next Saturday, Tex had a grand time buying magazines and items in Mr. Rivers' General Supply and Feed Store. What wasn't spent at the River's went towards ice cream and sodas at the Drug Store across the street.

It was in the Drug Store that he overheard a conversation between Doc Hammerstein and a fancy looking dude he hadn't seen before. Tex had heard some of the rumors that a wealthy Easterner by the name of Cabot had bought out several ranchers east of La Flor, the sum total of the acreage rumored to be about 20,000 acres. Locals had been talking for weeks about Cabot, speculating on why he'd purchased all this land and what he was planning to do with it. Some folks thought Cabot had come into his money by marrying a wealthy eastern woman, while others speculated he had made it in the stock market, buying shares of stock of companies that had plummeted in value during the Great Market Crash of 1929.

Mr. Cabot seemed to be in intense conversation with Doc Hammerstein. "Thank you, Mr. Hammerstein," he was saying. "I wanted you to meet Reggie and understand that he can purchase items for me on credit. I do wish you had a delivery system as a part of your store operations here, but I see that you don't have the resources for such an operation. Most of the supplies we will need will be first aid items and some household goods that the General Store doesn't carry. I haven't appointed a foreman yet, but when I do, you should honor his requests as well.

Reggie piped up, "Dad, that's going to include some sodas and ice cream right?"

"Yes son, it will, but don't overdo it, understand?"

"Yes Dad." Reggie smirked.

Tex, overhearing their dialogue instantly knew that he didn't want to pursue a friendship with a spoiled rich kid. Doc smiled at Mr. Cabot and nodded in understanding. The two Cabots left the Drug Store, passing Buckshot, who entered looking for Tex.

"Come on boy, we have to get moving."

On the ride back to the ranch Tex filled Buckshot in on the Cabot's conversation with Doc Hammerstein. Buckshot listened with interest but made no comments. However, the boy's dialogue did not fall upon deaf ears.

10

The Miguel Garcia Band was coming to La Flor! This was one of the most popular bands in all of Texas. Their music was a blend of Mexican and Country Western, and appealed to all ages.

In those days there was no such thing as "trick or treat" on Halloween. It was all trick, with the tricks being done to people's cars and homes. During the previous Halloween, tricksters poured tar on Doc Hammerstein's front porch, dumped muddy water all over Judge Byron's car, and let the air out of the Sheriff's vehicle.

A band concert would provide a wholesome Halloween diversion. The Garcia Band was renowned for its lively dance music, and merchants expected that people as far away as Del Rio would attend. Beer would be available, so Sheriff Mitchell believed he and Lonesome Pine would be busy. Fuzzy Tinker was sent over to the fairgrounds to assist those who were constructing a dance floor in any way he could. The festivities would start around sundown and last until midnight.

While not required, attendees were encouraged to wear costumes. There would be some prizes awarded to the best overall costume. At the River's house, Kathy and her mother were hard at work designing and preparing her costume. "Just think, Kathy," her mother said, "if you win, your picture will be in the newspaper! Is your friend Mary Boone coming to the concert?"

"I think so, mother!" she replied, "but I don't think she's going to be any competition for me!"

"Why so?" her mother asked.

"Mother, have you seen those pimples on her face? She's very self-conscious and embarrassed about them."

"Kathy," her mother replied, "She's a lovely girl with a beautiful smile and pretty blonde hair. Those pimples won't last long. I hope you keep her for a friend. Now let's get back to work on your costume."

At the S-> ranch, Betsy was discussing the Halloween affair with Tex. "The Garcia Band is one of the best in Texas; I'm sure you will enjoy their music. Why don't you want to go? You know some of the kids in La Flor—I know you've met some from the church."

"It's not that, Aunt Betsy. It's just that I don't know how to dance. I don't mind listening to the music, but I'm just not into this Halloween stuff."

"Tex, I'm disappointed in you. Jesse is not all excited about going either, but he's going for me. Besides, people will notice if we're not there!"

Buckshot had been looking for Tex and heard Betsy's comment upon entering the house. "That's right!" he said, "Don't forget the concert committee asked Judge Bryan to MC the best costume contest and he's asked me to be one of the judges. Tex, this is something you and Betsy can help with by scouting the crowd and giving me your opinions."

Down at the jail, the Sheriff's wife, Mrs. Mitchell, was busy as well. After talking it over with Fuzzy, he agreed to get dressed in a clown costume and hand out candy to the children as they came to the concert.

A festive mood permeated the town. Fall was in the air, and the weather was cool. And though the moon was only half full, its glow provided sufficient light for walking about the fairgrounds. The Garcia Band arrived just before the sun began to set and were busy moving instruments and equipment into position on the stage.

Some of the local Mexicans had brought their guitars and were sitting together singing and playing their music. Miguel Garcia often times invited local musicians to join him on stage at his concerts, which contributed to his popularity with audiences. Many folks came hoping he would invite them on stage.

People were continuing to arrive when the band began to play at eight o'clock. The Mexican and Texas Western music was conservative and pleasant. They played continuously for about two hours, until Judge Bryan marched out on stage to announce the intermission. The audience clapped heartily for one of their favorite townsmen. "Ladies and Gentlemen," he smiled as he gestured for quiet, "the moment you have been waiting for has arrived! The judges have given me their votes for best costumes. Ribbons will be awarded to the first and second place contestants. These prizes will be awarded to the two gentlemen and ladies whom the judges have chosen." He looked at the slips of paper and began coughing. "This is most unusual," he said, "in fact, this has never happened before! Would Miss Kathy Rivers, Mr. Reggie Cabot and Miss Carman Ruiz and her brother Miguel, please join me here on the stage." The crowd was hushed, followed by a murmur of excited voices, and then loud applause. Kathy led the way, followed by two Mexican youths and Reggie, who seemed to want to stay as far away from the Latino couple as possible.

"Ladies and Gentlemen, our winners for first place are for all four of these fine young people. The judges decided that there would be no runners up tonight." No Mexican had ever won the award before and at this announcement loud whoops were heard, and children began jumping up and down and clapping. Kathy smiled politely as she received her award and left the stage followed by Reggie. Mr. and Mrs. Rivers met their daughter just off the stage and gave her a big hug. Reggie, who was beautifully dressed in all white cowboy attire left to go get a soda. He was quickly followed by several of his school mates who came over to congratulate him. Reggie was obviously not overjoyed about tying with a "Mexican". He said little in response to the congratulations, and calmly walked over to the refreshment stand. He looked more like he was eighteen than his actual age of fifteen, so he was not questioned when he ordered a beer.

Intermission ended and the band began again with livelier tunes than before. Miguel Garcia announced that they would be playing dance tunes and everyone was invited to join in. They skillfully blended their own repertoire of Mexican songs and dances with those favored by the Texas ranchers, among which were the Pony Step, the Western Swing and the Push-Pull. By the time they got around to playing Cotton Eye Joe everyone in the crowd was having a wild, happy time.

Kathy had danced with Reggie briefly after the intermission but soon left to go home with her parents. When they were leaving her mother asked if she enjoyed dancing with Reggie. Kathy looked thoughtful, "He's OK, but he's pretty big for his britches and I think he had had a beer or two."

Mrs. Rivers replied, "Well don't take Reggie too seriously. After all, you both did place first in the costume contest, and his father has high social standing in the community."

Tex and the Steels remained at the concert because both Buckshot and Betsy were members of the festival committee. When Tex saw Kathy with Reggie, he decided to avoid both of them. He wandered around enjoying the music and watching the people. Then he encountered a girl wearing a nurse costume who, like himself, had not participated in the dancing. The two young people appeared to gravitate toward each other and seated themselves on a corner of the bleachers and began talking. This chance introduction was how Tex Hall met Mary Boone.

At the opposite end of the bleachers sat Fuzzy Tinker in his clown costume, wearing a top hat painted orange. He was tapping his feet in time to the music and appeared to be enjoying himself. Suddenly Reggie Cabot appeared, walking with a swagger, moved in part by the several beers he had consumed as well as his pride in winning an award for his costume. As he looked around, he felt quite superior to these local buffoons. He spotted Tex sitting with Mary at one end of the bleachers and noticed Fuzzy at the other end. The first thing he tried to do was to strike up a conversation with Tex and Mary.

"Hello, my pretty little chickadee," he said to Mary, "wouldn't you rather have a conversation with me than that illiterate yokel" gesturing toward Tex, "you are sitting with?"

"No, I would not!" answered Mary, tossing her head. At that Tex stood up slowly and deliberately and looked Reggie in the eye.

Without further comment, Reggie walked to the other end of the bleachers and began to heckle Fuzzy. "Hey, you with the stupid orange hat, are you some kind of a clown?" As a dog will put his head down in submission, Fuzzy looked down at the ground and said nothing. The heckling continued. "Aren't you that dimwit who sleeps down at the jail?" Reggie badgered. Fuzzy remained silent. "Not talking, aye, well I know how to get you to speak to one of your better's!" barked Reggie as he snatched the orange top hat from Fuzzy's head. This did provoke a response from Fuzzy! It made him angry.

"Give me back that hat! It belongs to Mrs. Mitchell!" yelled Fuzzy, as he started to rise. With that Reggie laughed and pushed Fuzzy back into the bleachers. Fuzzy fell with a thud to the ground. Immediately Tex responded and ran to help Fuzzy up from the ground.

"Reggie, give Fuzzy back his hat!" he commanded.

"You illiterate clod, make me!" Reggie snarled, slapping Tex across the face with his open hand. It was a solid blow, and Tex's nose began to bleed, but the blood from his nose was not nearly as red as the fire in his eyes.

His father had done that to him once and Tex had sworn it would never happen again. Yet, here this stranger had done the same thing. With volcanic fury, Tex attacked Reggie. His hard work at the S-> ranch had put Tex in top physical condition; on the other hand, Reggie was out of shape and soft from his life of self-indulgence.

Wham! Tex's left fist hit Reggie in the stomach just below his sternum. He followed the blow with a right to Reggie's face, staggering him. Tex hit

Reggie again in the stomach, doubling him over. Reggie went to his knees and threw up all over his beautiful white costume.

"Give that hat back to Fuzzy!" snarled Tex. He was about to administer the coup-de-gras when a pair of very strong arms grabbed him from behind. These arms belonged to Sheriff Lee Mitchell.

"What's going on here, boy?" the Sheriff demanded.

Fuzzy spoke up first saying, "That man talked mean to me and took my hat!"

"I was just trying to get him" said Tex pointing at Reggie, "to return that orange hat to Fuzzy!"

"That's true!" said a quiet feminine voice. Mary appeared to confirm the stories of Tex and Fuzzy.

"I think you two boys will need to come over to the jailhouse while I call your parents," said the Sheriff gruffly. He grasped each boy by the upper arm and marched them down to the jailhouse. Sheriff Mitchell knew who Tex was, but for public consumption, he decided to treat each boy equally.

Once inside the jailhouse, the Sheriff seated the boys on a bench in the hallway just outside his office. As he walked away, the Sheriff overheard Reggie tell Tex he'd get even with him. Reggie's comment did not sit well with the Sheriff, and he walked back into the hall.

"Son," he said to Reggie, "I believe you were the one who provoked this entire affair. Lonesome, would you go and get Mr. Steel and have him come here?" It was only a matter of minutes before Buckshot appeared, looking less than pleased. Sheriff Mitchell gave him a brief explanation of the incident and suggested he take Mary and Tex home. Tex went out the door with Buckshot, knowing it would be a very long ride back to the ranch.

Meanwhile, the Sheriff had placed a phone call to Reggie's father. "Mr. Cabot, the Sheriff began, "this is Sheriff Mitchell, here in La Flor. Your son has been involved in a fight. He is now in my custody here at the jail. You'll need to come and pick him up. I'll only release him to your custody."

"What are you talking about Sheriff? Reggie has his own car and can drive himself home. He's not so seriously injured that he can't do that, is he?"

"Mr. Cabot, I will repeat what I just said: we will release Reggie to your custody whenever you decide to come get him. He will remain here until then. Is that clear, Mr. Cabot?"

"Perfectly clear. This means I have to drive about forty miles to come get him. This is very inconvenient!" With that Cabot slammed the phone into the receiver.

On the way home, things were very quiet in the Steel's car. Finally, Buckshot broke the silence. "Tex, what I understand is that this Reggie fellow was harassing Fuzzy and you stepped in to help him. Is that correct?"

"Yes sir, that's correct." Tex answered.

"And this Reggie fellow slapped you across the face! Did you do anything to make him do that?"

"I told him to give Fuzzy back his hat! He hit me and then I went after him!"

Buckshot paused as if he was thinking the matter over, then said, "Betsy, you know what, I think Tex reacted just fine. If I'd been in his shoes, I'd have done the same thing! There are times when a man has to take a stand for what he believes is right."

Betsy responded, "Yes, Jesse I know you'd have done the same. Tex, I'm sorry this lovely evening ended on such a sour note!"

"Oh Aunt Betsy, it wasn't all that bad. It could have been worse if I'd lost the fight. I did meet a girl named Mary Boone. She is a friend of Kathy's and we had a nice time talking and drinking cokes together. One thing for sure, I'll be ready for bed when we get home!"

11

November arrived and the leaves began to lose their color. The weather at night became especially chilly. Dusty was almost full size now and Buckshot's attention since early October had been focused on the dog's training. This was rapidly producing good results.

The weather became suitable for marketing some of the S-> Ranch cattle and sheep. Buckshot was also looking forward to getting some meat in his large freezer. To do this, he would need some help. He decided to telephone his brother-in-law, Jim Rivers, to inquire about hiring a couple of hands to help with the slaughtering and marketing of the cattle. Rivers informed him that a couple of men had recently arrived in town looking for work. Both had just returned from Spain, having been discharged from the Lincoln Brigade. Rivers said one of them was helping him in the store, and the other had found temporary work at the stables.

"Do they have wheels?" Buckshot asked.

"I think so," replied Jim, "the horse hand sleeps in one of the stalls at the stable. He's a big man and they call him Bull. I think the one helping me sleeps in the back of his truck. He goes by the name Shorty. They need extra work and would probably be fine for your job. If they don't work out, just send them back and I'll try to find you someone else."

"Thanks, Jim. After you've talked with them give me a call and I'll make the arrangements with Shorty."

The next day Rivers contacted Buckshot and the arrangements were made for the men to report on the following Monday, the seventh of November, for work at the S-> arrow ranch. Tex had already left to walk his trap line that morning, hoping to be back in time to witness the slaughtering of the hogs. He had never seen anything like a slaughtering before. Three hogs were to be put down, although Buckshot didn't elaborate on which ones.

Around mid morning, Tex returned to the ranch house to find Betsy in the back yard hanging out the wash. As he approached, Tex waved and held up his harvest so she could see. It was a large gray fox. She waved back smiling. Tex continued walking on to the corral and hog pens. The two hands were in the pen. They had caught a hog and were trying to tie a rope to its hind legs. Buckshot was not in sight. Tex suddenly realized the pig they were intending to put down was Matilida.

He reacted immediately. He considered Matilda to be his property; besides, Matilda was the first gentle thing or animal he had encountered upon arrival at the Steel's ranch.

"Stop!" he screeched, "You can't do that! That's *my* hog!"

The men just looked at him and laughed.

"This is the hog we were told to put down, and this is the hog we're going to put down," Shorty growled.

"No you're not!" yelled Tex, throwing the fox carcass at the larger of the two men and hitting him in the neck. Instantly, the big man jumped up, his eyes blazing with anger.

He almost leaped over the fence as he growled, "I'm going to teach you a lesson kid! Don't nobody do what you just done to me!" He managed to grab Tex and yanked him off the ground, holding him by the collar with one hand. Betsy heard the commotion and flew to the rescue,

"Stop!" she screamed "You put down that boy, now!"

The man snarled and made a motion to hit Tex, but Betsy's screams caused him to pause. Suddenly, Buckshot reappeared on the scene, "Put that boy down!" he commanded.

"What's going on here, Betsy!"

"Those men were going to slaughter Matilda and I stopped them." Tex answered for Betsy. Betsy's eyes snapped, "That's Tex's pet, and nothing is going to happen to that pig on this ranch!"

Buckshot knew he was in the doghouse big time. "Men, you heard what the lady said, untie that hog."

The larger man named Bull threw his hat to the ground, exclaiming, "We quit! No rotten kid is going to hit me with a dead animal. We'll collect our pay now, Mr. Steel, and then Shorty and me will be leaving."

Shorty added, "And kid, you watch out—don't never come near us, do you hear?" Tex looked him in the eye, but remained silent as the two men departed.

With his hired hands gone, the job of butchering the hogs and scraping off their hair fell to Buckshot. It was mighty quiet around the barn and ranch house that evening. Tex remained at the barn trying to be of help. Tex thought he was in the doghouse with Buckshot. Buckshot knew he was in the doghouse with Betsy. All three of them had a good case of the miseries.

Later that evening at the barn, Buckshot broke the silence, "Son, we all made some mistakes today. The best we can do is learn from our mistakes, don't you think? I sure made the mistake of leaving those men unsupervised."

"Yes sir," Tex agreed politely. "I owe Aunt Betsy an apology. I shouldn't have thrown the dead fox at Bull."

"Well Tex, it looks like we both have some apologizing to do. Let's clean up here, march down to the ranch house and set things right with the boss. I think we really upset her today."

"Buckshot," Tex said, "I'm so sorry, but you told me that Matilda was to be my special hog and I believed you."

"Yes son, I did and she is. Those men didn't listen to me very well. I didn't tell them to put Matilda down."

The old cowboy and the young cowpoke marched to the ranch house and did their best to smooth the ruffled feathers of the leading lady on the ranch. Luckily, they succeeded.

A day or two passed after Shorty and Bull left. Betsy answered the phone to discover an excited Ruth Rivers on the other end of the line.

"Guess what, Betsy!" the voice on the phone crackled with static. "We've been invited to dinner over at the Cabot's ranch—our whole family! Mr. Cabot also invited Doc and Polly Hammerstein. He says he wants to get to know some of the prominent local folks. Did he invite you all?"

"No, Ruth," Betsy chuckled "I guess we're not prominent enough! But I think that is very nice and I hope you all have an enjoyable evening. Let me know all about it!"

"I will" promised Ruth.

Betsy relayed this conversation to Jesse, whose comment was terse. "Sounds like that Cabot fellow hasn't forgotten the bout his darling boy had with Tex."

The next phone call from Ruth Rivers came the day following the Cabot dinner. Her excitement in relating the events to her sister was evident.

"How was your evening?" Betsy inquired.

"Oh it was lovely," answered Ruth "but on the way home Kathy told us something a little disturbing."

"What was that?"

"Kathy said that when Reggie took her back to the family room to listen to phonograph records, Reggie pinned her against a wall and tried to kiss her."

"He didn't!" Betsy was shocked.

"That's what Kathy told us. She was very distressed over Reggie's behavior. I don't think that boy is to be trusted. We won't be accepting any more invitations to the Cabot place."

A few days before, Betsy had discussed with Buckshot her idea of inviting the Rivers for Thanksgiving, which was only about two weeks away. "They've had us to their place several times and we owe it to them."

Jesse had wholeheartedly agreed to this arrangement, so before Betsy and Ruth's phone conversation ended, she popped the Thanksgiving invitation.

"It sounds like a lovely idea," said Ruth, "I'll check with James and if there's a conflict I'll let you know, otherwise we'd love to come."

Betsy smiled as she hung up the phone and went to find Buckshot. "Jesse, I've invited the Rivers for Thanksgiving. We have everything we need except the turkey. We could omit the turkey, but if you and Tex can scout one up for us, it would make for a perfect occasion."

12

Saturday before Thanksgiving was a big day for La Flor merchants and townsfolk. Buckshot, Betsy and Tex went to town for supplies, gossip and the bustling social atmosphere. Tex wanted a few of the latest cowboy stories and an ice cream cone. Betsy had Thanksgiving on her mind and Buckshot wanted to round up some feed for the hogs and milk cows.

Tex was perched on a corner stool in the Drugstore, well into the first stages of ice cream cone demolishment, when Sheriff Mitchell walked in. He saw the empty stool next to Tex and sat down.

"You got room for an old lawman, Tex?"

"You bet, Sheriff!"

The two began chatting about local folks and happenings on the S-> Ranch. Sheriff Lee asked about Buckshot and Tex's trapping successes. Tex's replies were positive and upbeat. The boy had known for some time that both the Sheriff and Buckshot had served in the Marines in France, during the great war of 1917. Buckshot would never talk about his military experiences, so Tex decided to try and pry some information from the Sheriff. He wanted to learn all he could about his hero.

"Sheriff Mitchell, you and Buckshot were in the war in France together, right? How was it being in the Army and all around Europe?"

Now Tex, being inexperienced and unknowledgeable about military matters, did not realize that asking the preceding question to a former Marine was sure to trigger a creative response.

"Son, we weren't in the Army, we served in the United States Marines! We were the Devil Dogs of the Devil Dogs! Your Buckshot was a machine gunner in my platoon. He was one of the best, and a real hero." Sheriff Mitchell looked thoughtful, "The night before the war ended, he sure proved his true worth. We were ordered to cross a large river called the Meuse. It was to be a night crossing and, as it turned out, our mission took place just hours before the war officially ended. It was really dark that night. I had just finished crossing the river when some enemy soldier put a bullet in my right shoulder. Buckshot was nearby when I was hit and reacted instantly. He grabbed me as I fell back and dragged me to the river's edge to safety. He was hit in the leg while dragging me out of the water. Thankfully the Germans surrendered the next day, November 11th, 1918. Our wounds weren't too bad, which was the biggest blessing of the whole deal." The Sheriff grinned and put a hand on Tex's shoulder, "Now we're here in La Flor and we have you to help us, which makes for another blessing!" Tex smiled broadly at the Sheriff's last statement as the door opened and Buckshot walked in.

Tex excitedly relayed his new found knowledge of Buckshot's heroic actions. "He said you were a real hero to drag him out of the water to safety!" The boy's words tumbled over each other.

"Well, it wasn't much, Tex. Sheriff Mitchell was our sergeant and if something happened to him, I would've had to take charge." Buckshot winked at Tex.

"What was your rank, Buckshot?" Tex questioned.

"Oh, I was only a corporal."

"Well, you were the best corporal we had!" said the sheriff, as the two men quickly changed the subject. Tex could hardly wait until he saw Aunt Betsy to tell her he'd just learned Buckshot and Sheriff Mitchell were real war heroes.

"When I grow up, I want to be a Marine, just like them!" he thought.

With the big thanksgiving feast only four days away, Buckshot decided to devote as much time as possible hunting for the elusive turkey. Tex had reported seeing some down near the creek in the vicinity of his trap lines. On Monday morning, Buckshot set out early by himself, but was back at mid-day empty handed. Betsy and Tex were in the kitchen when he arrived.

"I heard a gobble about midmorning, about a mile away," he related to them. "There's a field up on the northwest side of the creek. We tried to do some planting there, but it was too dry last year and didn't produce a worthwhile crop. It's probably a place that turkeys would like. Tex, why don't you come with me tomorrow, and bring along the 20 gauge shotgun? Who knows, we might see more than one turkey."

That night the boy could hardly sleep. He had never been on a turkey hunt before and had no idea what to expect, especially since Buckshot hadn't provided any details.

About two hours before daybreak, Buckshot rousted a sleepy boy from his bed. The two hunters dressed quickly, ate some cold cereal, and stuffed a couple of peanut butter sandwiches into their pockets, before moving quietly out of the house.

Buckshot walked so quickly that Tex occasionally had to run to keep up. When they reached the creek and turned left, Buckshot slowed to a quiet deliberate pace, giving Tex a chance to catch his breath. They walked until they reached a spot where the brush lessened. Tex now could see a field stretching out ahead.

"We'll sit down here, and I'll see if I can get a gobble," said Buckshot. They sat quietly a few feet behind the edge of the brush. Buckshot put his hand to the side of his mouth and hooted like an owl. "Tex," he whispered, "turkeys hate owls, and if the turkey gets mad enough, sometimes he'll gobble at the owl." No gobbles responded. The man and boy sat quietly as the dawn faded. Suddenly they heard a very quiet "yelp, yelp, yelp!"

"Shh, that's a hen," Buckshot whispered. "The flock must be nearby. Don't move at all, just stay still." As they listened they could hear the flap of wings.

"They are flying down off the roost now," Buckshot whispered "keep very still!"

Then another series of clucks and yelps echoed across the field.

"They're up on the ridge behind us." Buckshot continued with his narration.

Suddenly, with no sound at all, they saw a large bird fly from the ridge to the field, almost directly over their heads.

"Turkey!" Buckshot whispered excitedly. His gun was in position as he whispered to Tex, "Get ready!" A second turkey flew in the trace of the first. Buckshot fired, but missed. He remained focused and began to reload. "If another bird flies, you shoot too!"

A third bird flew and both hunters fired. The turkey dropped like a stone.

"We got one!" Buckshot said with a smile. "Let's see if there are any others." Both hunters remained in position. Sure enough, a fourth bird flew, and Tex raised his gun and fired.

"I hit him!" He exclaimed as Buckshot fired a backup shot. The majestic bird fell from the air.

"All right, Tex—good work! We've had us a turkey hunt!" Buckshot was grinning like a true Texan, from ear to ear. "Betsy is going to be very pleased. We've not only hunted us up a Thanksgiving turkey, but a Christmas one as well! Let's head for the house."

Spirits were high in the Steel home that evening. As far as Aunt Betsy was concerned, the menfolk still had their work cut out for them in order to be ready for the big day. Not only did the birds need to be plucked and cleaned, but the house needed their full attention as well. Betsy expected it to be clean as a whistle. The table had to be set just so, and after Betsy conducted an inspection of the grounds around the house, her troops were going to be raking, cleaning, and window washing. At one point Tex asked Buckshot if the preparation phase would ever end.

"Son," he said, "not until the guests arrive. You can be sure of that! She'll probably ease up just long enough for us to bathe and put on some clean duds."

"Will Kathy be coming?" the boy asked.

"I expect so; I think they are bringing her horse."

"Can I wear my spurs?"

"Well, maybe after dinner when you all go outside. That'll be an OK time for the spurs, especially if you and Kathy go riding."

13

Thanksgiving Day arrived. Light rain during the night had made the ground moist and the temperature cooler. Dinner was planned for one o'clock that afternoon, and the Rivers family arrived about noontime. This allowed time to unload Kathy's horse from the trailer, and bring in some of the various food items Ruth had agreed to bring for their enjoyment. Nuts, dried fruit and apples, as well as pumpkin and apple pies, were unloaded into the kitchen. Betsy had already organized the rest of the meal, consisting of turkey, venison, hogs head cheese, and mashed and sweet potatoes. In addition, she had prepared dressing, gravy, collard greens, biscuits, iced tea and coffee, all of which were placed either on the dining table, sideboard, or kitchen table. Everyone would serve him or herself, going from station to station.

After all were seated, Buckshot said a short prayer of thanks to God for the bountiful meal and beautiful people gracing the table. Everyone went to work in a brave attempt to eat the mounds of food. It was a happy meal, with lots of conversation and laughter.

When the meal ended, Buckshot and Jim Rivers went out on the porch to talk and smoke the Thanksgiving cigars Jim had brought. Timmy Rivers wandered about the house until Kathy and Tex volunteered to take him outside to play catch. They played, until Timmy finally excused himself to go into the house.

Kathy then suggested that she and Tex saddle up the horses and go for a ride. Tex was ready! This time wearing his spurs was for a good purpose!

The youngsters decided to ride out to the north fields where the cattle were grazing, and the border fence of the Steel and Schultz ranches was located. The Schultz's were good neighbors and friends; their ranch house was about five miles from the Steels. A gate had been placed in the fence line so that the two families could visit each other. Visits by car would have added another five miles to the trip. The gate not only made the trip much shorter and quicker, but it was also useful for moving cattle and collecting strays.

The girl and the boy rode out happily, their stomachs full. The day was sunny and cool, and Tex began talking about the cows.

"Buckshot just released a real nice bull out here and I wanted to show him to you.—I wonder where the cattle are." He said looking around.

Tex and Kathy followed the fence line until they reached the gate for the Schultz's ranch. To their surprise, the gate was open.

"Maybe the cattle went through this gate. I wonder who opened it?" said Tex "Buckshot and I were up here a few days ago, and the gate was closed. The Schultzs sold their place to Mr. Cabot recently and moved away. Who opened this gate? Let's keep riding towards the Schultz's old ranch house. Maybe we'll see our cows. If we do, we can move them back to our ranch, and Buckshot will be real pleased."

They continued riding in an easterly direction. Before long they heard the mooing of cattle. Straight ahead was a small rise in the ground with a few scrub oaks on it. They rode up onto the rise and passed among the trees. Down below, almost a mile away, they saw the cattle with two strange riders herding them along.

Kathy was riding only slightly ahead of Tex when she turned and asked, "Who are those men, Tex? Do you know them?"

Tex answered "I can't tell right now; we need to ride a little closer!"

Kathy responded "I don't like the looks of this. Shouldn't we ride back for my Dad and Uncle Jesse?"

As the youngsters rode down for a better look, the riders turned and rode towards them. One was riding a mule and the other, a much larger man, was seated on a big brown horse. Suddenly Tex realized who they were.

The taller one was Bull and the man on the mule was Shorty, the two men Buckshot had hired to help with the hog slaughtering. Tex remembered Shorty's threat after he had thrown the fox at Bull. The riders were closing the distance rapidly.

"Kathy!" Tex yelled. "We're in big trouble! That's Bull and Shorty! Let's get out of here fast! Ride for the ranch! Now!"

Tex whirled his horse about, but Kathy's reaction was a bit slower. She had moved slightly ahead of Tex as they were riding towards the herd. Her decision to turn was poorly executed. She pulled back hard on the reins, her horse reared, and while turning, went down. Kathy fell with the horse, her leg pinned under the horse's side.

She cried out, "I'm hurt!" Tex saw the accident and made a quick decision. He knew he had only one choice—to ride for the ranch and get Buckshot's help.

Kathy was still on the ground when the two bad men rode up. Bull yelled, "Shorty, get the girl, I'm going after the boy! I owe that little pinhead one." He kicked his horse into a full gallop and the race was on.

Tex was riding Star and the cowpony was fast. However, Bull still managed to pull up alongside Tex. He tried to reach out and grab him, but Tex's reflexes were quicker, and he deftly turned Star's head, whirling the horse back towards the ranch. Bull tried to rein his horse in and make the same turn but Star was faster. Tex's lightning fast movements caused Bull to lose his balance. Those precious seconds were all that were needed for Tex to regain the lead. As he dashed through the Steel/Shultz gate, Bull reined in his horse, giving up the chase as he turned and headed back to Shorty and the girl.

Kathy was still on the ground with what appeared to be a broken leg. The fact that the young girl was hurt didn't seem to bother Shorty or Bull. Shorty was still sitting on his mule when Bull returned. Bull roughly picked up Kathy and threw her over Shorty's mule, face down. She screamed with pain.

"Well, pretty girl," Shorty growled as he held her in place, "you're going with us. You'll be good insurance. We've already got that little Cabot snot-nose, Reggie, back at the Schultz house. Good thing Shorty went over to the Cabot place early this morning and tricked the little pinhead into riding over here with him to meet his father."

Meanwhile, Tex had made good time returning to the S-> Ranch. As he rode up to the front gate of the house, he jumped off, screaming "Buckshot! Buckshot! Aunt Betsy! They've got Kathy!" Hearing his cries, Buckshot, Betsy, Jim and Ruth Rivers came streaming out of the house.

"What's happened? What's going on?" Buckshot asked the frightened boy.

"Those two men—those two men you hired to kill the pigs"—Tex was gasping for breath, "Shorty and Bull—they have our cows and they have Kathy. Her horse fell with her; I think she's hurt!"

"Holy mackerel!" Jim exclaimed. "What are we going to do?"

Buckshot's demeanor suddenly changed from gentle rancher to Marine warrior, as the former corporal took charge.

"Jim, go call the Sheriff, tell him I'm riding to the Schultz house. Hopefully I can make those fools hole up there. Also, get hold of Doctor Simons and tell him to drive here and wait for me to call. Get Mitchell to drive to the Schultz house and look for me, he'll probably see my Grey first. Tell him to stop near the Grey and plan on walking in from there. I'll probably try and work my way around to the rear of the Schultz house. And Jim, please stay here with the ladies. You all wait for our phone call!"

With that, Buckshot ran to the barn, shotgun in hand, to saddle his horse and ride to the Schultz house. Once mounted, he put Grey into a steady loping gait. The horse responded beautifully and moved like greased silk.

The sun was beginning to sink below the horizon as Buckshot approached the ranch. He noticed a mule and brown horse tied outside the house, and assumed Shorty and Bull were inside with Kathy. He didn't know Reggie Cabot was also a prisoner inside. Buckshot saw cattle spread out all over the nearby fields and noticed that several carried his brand. "What those two eight-balls are doing is crazy" thought Buckshot, "What could they be thinking?" He shook his head and mumbled to himself "This guy Cabot must have been nuts to have hired them."

Inside the Schultz house, Bull was on a rampage, angry, and desperate. Shorty sat quietly looking through the rear windows for movement with steely eyes. Reggie Cabot was tied up in the corner whimpering. They had tied Kathy's hands and she was lying on the floor making no sound. She was hurt, but she was proving to be a tough, gritty girl.

Finally, Bull couldn't stand the silence any longer. He went to the telephone and dialed the Steel's phone number.

Betsy answered the ring. "Is that you, Mrs. Steel?" Bull growled. "Let me speak to your man!"

"Jim," she whispered, "Take the phone. It's one of them, he will think he's talking to Jesse!"

Jim took the phone and placed his hand over the mouthpiece in an effort to sound more like Buckshot.

"Look, Mr. Steel, we've got the girl, that little Cabot puke and your cattle. You can have all of 'em back for ten thousand dollars! If we see any lawmen coming, we'll kill both the boy and girl, understood?" There was an ominous click and the line went dead.

Jim tried to sound calm, "Betsy, Ruth—That was Bull. They want ten thousand dollars ransom or they'll hurt the kids. I'm praying Mitchell hasn't left yet. I'm going to call and fill him in on the situation."

He dialed the phone for the Sheriff's office. Fuzzy Tinker answered, "Fuzzy—has the Sheriff left yet?"

"No sir, he's getting in his car right now."

"O.K., run out there and fetch him to this phone, NOW! Tell him I need to speak with him!"

A minute or so later, Sheriff Lee Mitchell was on the phone receiving the latest report from Jim Rivers.

"Ransom, eh! Two kids! Okay, that changes things slightly, but we'll deal with it. Thanks, Jim, don't worry, Buckshot and I will handle this." Sheriff Mitchell hung up the phone and went outside.

His deputy, "Lonesome" Pine, was waiting, armed with his own rifle and shotgun.

"Get in, Lonesome, and let's go!" Mitchell revved up the engine and the car responded. It wasn't until they had driven some distance out of town that Lee and Lonesome realized there was another person in the back seat. It was Fuzzy Tinker.

"Fuzzy, what the dickens are you doing back there?" The sheriff growled with annoyance upon noticing his presence.

"I'm going with you, Sheriff. Maybe I can do some good."

"You should not have come," Mitchell responded, "but maybe you can help. And Fuzzy, the best way you can help is to not talk and just do what I say, Okay?"

"Yes sir!"

While Buckshot's horse was galloping toward the Schultz's house, his mind was racing at the speed of light. He mentally reviewed his expectations, options, and alternatives for a course of action. It would be early twilight when he got there. He remembered that only a few days before, he and Betsy were sitting on the front porch admiring the full moon. The moon would be about three-quarters full now. This was plenty of moonlight to see the "enemy". The moonlight could both benefit his movement but could hinder it as well. The two in the cabin would be able to see out and have a clear view of the open spaces.

"On second thought," he mused, "Maybe I better wait for the Sheriff. He wouldn't know exactly where I would be and that could be more hazardous than dealing with those two lobos inside." So Buckshot halted his horse about a hundred yards from the house and waited.

The Sheriff's vehicle came in with lights off and stopped upon seeing Buckshot's horse. Buckshot called in a low voice, "Lee, it's Buckshot. I'm over here under this tree!" He stepped out of the shadows.

"How long have you been here?" Sheriff asked.

"Not long. Both of their animals are tied out front and you can see their truck over to the left. There'll be too much moonlight for them to make a run for it. We've got them pinned inside."

Mitchell stepped out of his car and put his hands on his friend's shoulders saying, "O.K. Buckshot. Here's what we've got to do—I'm going to try and talk them into surrendering. In the meantime, Lonesome, you move out and cover the left side and left rear corner of the house. Buckshot, take Fuzzy with you and cover the right side and rear of the house. Both of you watch that back door. Don't forget to keep an eye on each other, and don't forget where Lonesome will be. My guess is if they come out the back door they'll try and circle around the left side. Lonesome can deal with that. Don't shoot unless you have to, and make sure you clearly identify the target. I'm going to get as close to the truck as I can and start talking. You should be able to hear me. Any questions? O.K. then, let's move out!"

"The Sarge has a good plan," thought Buckshot as he moved out.

Mitchell walked towards the house hoping to draw attention to himself and away from Buckshot, Lonesome and Fuzzy.

"Hey, you in the house! Can you hear me?" There was silence.

"We can," Shorty finally roared, "Did you bring the ten thousand dollars?"

"Shorty," the Sheriff called, "you and Bull—come on out now with your hands raised. Things will be a whole lot better for you if you just come out now." More silence.

"Then I think you forgot the ten grand," Bull sneered. "If you don't give us that ten grand, we're going to shoot these two kids we have in here."

Mitchell feigned surprise, "Two kids? Who are they Bull? Which kids do you have?"

Shooting the kids was a serious threat, and Bull was getting antsy. Sheriff Mitchell knew he needed to engage Shorty and Bull in extended conversation. He moved closer to the house. The door suddenly opened and Reggie appeared with Bull holding his arms. Reggie whimpered "Save us!" as Bull yanked him quickly back into the house. Mitchell could see the muzzle of a gun barrel in the window. "We have the girl too," Bull called. "You want to see her? Well then, we better see some greenbacks, and soon!"

"Bull, have you forgotten today is Thanksgiving? The banks are closed. We won't be able to get you the money until tomorrow. You don't need to hold two kids for ransom. Why don't you let one of them go now?"

"Two is better than one," Bull roared back. "You know the banker; go get him to open the bank and give you the money!"

"At least he's talking now. We're making progress," the Sheriff thought.

The Sheriff continued to talk to Bull, hoping the communication would soften Bull a bit. It didn't seem to be working however. It seemed to be a standoff. Mitchell began to worry; there had been no communication with Shorty. He continued his dialogue with Bull as an ominous thought crept into his mind, "Shorty hasn't said a word. He might be the tougher and more dangerous of the two hombres. He's probably the brains behind this whole episode!"

Night came on rather quickly. Thankfully there were no clouds in the sky and even though the moon was in its early rising stage, visibility was good. The moon favored Shorty, who had stationed himself to gain a clear view through both the rear window and the window on the right side of the house. He started suddenly when he noticed one figure trying to sneak through the sparse cover on his side of the house.

Lonesome was better able to conceal his movements having stationed himself as directed on the left side of the house. He was far enough back from the house that he had a partial view of its front and back sides. He knew the exact location of the Sheriff, and could easily back him up. However, he was unsure of where Buckshot and Fuzzy were exactly.

Shorty knew that there were at least two people outside the old Schultz house. One would be the sheriff, the other was probably Buckshot. He was beginning to realize that he and Bull were trapped unless they surrendered, or could take out the sheriff and some of his men.

"Surrender is not an option" said Shorty to himself. He decided to go after the man trying to creep around the backside of the house since this would be his easiest target. That man was Buckshot. He didn't know that Lonesome, the fourth man, was already in his assigned position at the left rear corner of the house. Shorty did not know Lonesome was part of the Sheriff's team. Shorty went to the back door and began to gently push it open. Because he was right handed, he wanted to expose himself only enough to see the man in the shadows creeping through the brush. Fuzzy saw the door begin to open and the dark figure of Shorty slide quietly out. He watched as Shorty's arm and gun went up pointed straight at Buckshot. Fuzzy was terrified and with no firearm, all he could do was to scream, "Watch out, Mr. Steel! Watch out! He's going to shoot!" With that Shorty pivoted slightly and fired. Fuzzy went down. As Fuzzy fell,

Buckshot reacted and fired at the flash of Shorty's gun. Shorty reacted and fired at Buckshot, hitting him in the side. Buckshot dropped down onto one knee.

As the shooting began, Lonesome moved quickly to cover Buckshot, but not in time to prevent Shorty from shooting Buckshot. When Lonesome saw Buckshot fall to his knee, he fired at the figure in the doorway. Shorty pitched forward and rolled over. Lonesome fired a second shot, and it was all over for Shorty Scroggs.

Lonesome left his position and quietly moved to the back side of the house, shielding himself next to the door which remained partially open. To his relief, Shorty's gun lay in plain sight well away from his body, so Lonesome left it there.

At the sound of the first shots, Bull panicked and whirled his large body around facing the front door. As he did so, the door crashed open under the weight and force of a charging six foot two, one-hundred-ninety-five pound, Sheriff, who ploughed into the big man with the force of an elephant. Bull's gun flew from his hand as he went down, but he quickly rolled and was on his feet in an instant.

Bull lunged towards the sheriff, his fists blazing. But the big man was no match for the agile and tough sheriff who dodged the first punch like a cat, and with his left fist hit Bull hard on his right cheek. Bull stumbled, and tried to regain his footing. "Pick on me now, Bull," the Sheriff taunted, "I'm no boy." The Sheriff backed Bull into the corner near where Kathy lay, pounding him as if he were a punching bag. Kathy rolled out of the way then with much effort, kicked Bull behind the knee with her one good leg. As his knee buckled, Bull went down and the fight was over.

Lonesome ran into the house with his gun at the ready, but Bull lay on the floor unmoving. "Keep him covered, Lonesome" the sheriff said calmly as he picked up his hat, "I'm going outside to see about Buckshot and Fuzzy."

Sheriff Lee returned shortly with Buckshot, who had sustained a grazing shot on his left side. The bleeding made it look worse than it was, although he did need immediate attention.

Buckshot spoke through his pain, "Lee, I think Fuzzy was shot—he went down back of the house. You'd better go see about him too."

The Sheriff quickly left to look for Fuzzy, and found him lying near the brush. Mitchell knelt down and placed his hand under Fuzzy's head. Fuzzy was barely alive. He had sustained a mortal wound in his chest and was going fast. He winced and grinned up at the Sheriff with a sad expression on his eyes, "Sheriff, did I do some good? I just wanted to do some good."

"Fuzzy, you done real good." the Sheriff spoke softly. With a faint smile, Fuzzy's eyes closed, and he was gone. The Sheriff felt a quiet stillness, broken only by the distant call of a whip-poor-will bird singing its mournful song. Lee Mitchell looked up to the heavens, listened, and thought "Fittin' and appropriate for poor Will "Fuzzy" Tinker." The Sheriff got up and walked slowly back towards the house to let Buckshot and the others know about Fuzzy.

Inside, Lonesome had handcuffed Bull's hands behind him and ordered him to lie face down on the floor. Both youngsters were untied, but Reggie was still blubbering. Finally, Kathy had had enough of Reggie. Her broken leg was causing extreme pain.

"Shut up, Reggie, and help Mr. Steel. Can't you see he's been hurt?"

Buckshot grinned at Kathy and took charge. "Yes Reggie, go and see if you can find a couple of dry towels, then help me over to the telephone."

There was a stool near the phone where Buckshot sat to call Betsy. Just as he started to dial the number the Sheriff walked in. "Buckshot, Fuzzy's gone, that bullet wound was mortal; he didn't make it."

"Too bad," said Buckshot grimly, "But at least the man can rest his soul knowing he saved the lives of these children, and you and me as well." Buckshot dialed his wife again. "Betsy, it's over," he said. Kathy has a broken leg, otherwise she's OK. I've been nicked a bit but I'm OK too. Is Doc Simmons there with you?"

"Yes," Betsy answered.

"Then have him bring Jim over in his car. You and Ruth can come over in the truck. We'll need it to transport our prisoner back to town. Also, Betsy, we're gonna need an undertaker. Shorty and Fuzzy are both dead. I'm sorry to be short, but I'll give you the details when you get here. Leave Tex at home to mind the ranch." Buckshot hung up the phone, and after repeated urging from Sheriff Mitchell, consented to lie on the floor.

All activity lasted until the early hours of the morning. Doctor Simons arrived and cleaned out Buckshot's wound. As the doctor poured iodine into the wound and began to sew it up, Buckshot gritted his teeth. He made no sound; after all, he had been a trained Marine, and his old unit leader 'Sergeant' Lee Mitchell was present.

Mitchell, on the other hand, looked a little green as he watched the doctor fix Buckshot's wound. He finally retreated to the stool by the phone and sat with his head in his hands. Betsy looked pale at the sight of her husband's injury but kept her cool as she helped the doctor. The Doctor tended to Kathy next, and splinted her leg, while her concerned parents comforted their brave daughter. The leg was fractured, but fortunately for her it was only a simple fracture that would heal quickly.

Lonesome, helped by Jim, loaded Fuzzy's body into the bed of the pickup and covered his face with a towel. Bull was escorted into the bed of the truck and tied securely to prevent any method of escape. A rope was tied around his neck and held by Lonesome as extra insurance. The undertaker carried Shorty Scroggs back to town in his vehicle. The Sheriff and Lonesome, with their prisoner and the body of Fuzzy Tinker, drove to the town jail. Reggie called his father, who sent someone for him.

Fuzzy was placed on his cot in the cell where he had slept. Bull was contained in the other end cell, pending charges and trial. The events of the day circulated around town like wildfire.

"Poor Fuzzy," many said "He was a hero."

"We'll miss him."

"A failure in life redeemed."

Services in both churches were conducted in memory of Will "Fuzzy" Tinker. He was laid to rest in the town cemetery, with many citizens attending.

The next day at the Steel ranch, Betsy surprised everyone by sleeping until about mid-morning. Tex hadn't awakened so early himself, but he was the first one up. Buckshot slept till almost noon and then proceeded to grump about being stiff and sore when he woke up.

"Now Jesse," Betsy said softly, "The doctor wants you to stay quiet for a few days and give that wound a chance to heal. He'll probably be calling Sunday afternoon, so you just stay put till then!"

"Yes ma'am," he smiled. "Do you think I could have a cup of coffee?" She smiled, relieved, and Tex added,

"Don't worry, Buckshot, Aunt Betsy and I can take care of everything until you are up and about."

"This was sure a Thanksgiving we'll never forget," he remarked as he stood quietly observing.

"Can I ask a question, Buckshot?" said the boy.

"Why of course, son."

"Over at the Schultz place, you seemed to know just what to do. Was it because you knew about fighting from the war in France? How did you know what to do?"

"The main thing in any difficult situation," he answered, "is to keep cool, observe what is happening, think, and do what needs to be done to solve the problem and get results. I learned that in France and used it here!"

"You are a real hero!" said the boy, "When I grow up, I want to be a soldier, just like you!"

"Marine!" answered Buckshot. "We're the best. Plan on being a Marine! You'll be a good one!"

"I will, Buckshot. I will."

14

By mid December it had become colder. Buckshot was up and about and things had about returned to normal. The Steels were just beginning to think about Christmas, excited about the prospect of sharing it with Tex. One day however, an unexpected phone call came for Buckshot.

"Hello Mr. Steel, this is Jake's father. I've returned home and I'm feeling much better now. How has my boy been doing?"

Buckshot was surprised, "Oh fine, sir. He's taken to this place like a duck to water. He's grown some and put on some muscle."

"Well, we'd like to have him home for Christmas. I've made arrangements for him to go to a military academy boarding school beginning in January. We need him home to get outfitted in his school uniforms and to pack his things for school. When can you bring him up?"

Buckshot was startled, "Well, sir, this is a bit of a surprise. I'd like to discuss this with my wife and call you back, if you don't mind.

"That will be fine. I'll expect your call tomorrow."

Jesse hung up the phone, turned to his wife who was beginning to fix lunch, and said quietly, "Betsy—do you know where Tex is?"

"I think he's still out on his trap lines. Should be back soon though."

"Well, come sit down. We need to talk." She joined him, guessing from the tone of his voice a serious discussion was about to ensue.

"Tex's father just called. He's back home from the hospital and wants the boy to come home. Asked how he was—never said a word of thanks. Damn it, I was looking forward to having him here for Christmas!"

The two were silent for a moment. "Oh, Lord," Betsy said, tears in her eyes. "I've come to love that boy, he's been a real joy to us." She continued, "Jesse, we can't be all sad, Tex has filled an important void in our lives. He came needing us and we needed him." She paused and placed her head on Buckshot's arm. "Buckshot, we have something new to look forward to."

"What's that?" he asked.

Betsy had an unusual look on her pretty face, "I've been waiting for the right time to tell you. God has blessed us again. We're going to have a baby—I'm pregnant!"

Buckshot turned white and his mouth fell almost to the floor.

"Close your jaw before you catch flies, man, and lend a hand." Betsy smirked as she rose to return to the kitchen. "We're having Christmas early this year! We've got Tex's presents to wrap, and a Christmas dinner to fix! We have a lot to do before he gets back." Buckshot stood there amazed, as a slow smile grew across his face. "Yes, ma'am!"

1951

"Easy men, easy," the voice commanded as they unbuckled the stretcher from the skids of the marine helicopter. "You're aboard the USS Consolation, Lieutenant. We're going to take good care of you here."

As this was taking place, the Petty officer on the ship's bridge was busy recording in the ship's log:

0900 June 20, 1951, Marine Helicopter HR-151 landed with one wounded. Crew off loaded Marine casualty. 0905 helicopter departed, destination Pusan, Korea.

Something was covering his eyes; he could not see. He tried moving his arms, but only the right arm moved slightly. The pain was intense. He had no feeling in his legs either. He faded into a deep sleep and began dreaming.

A scene appeared. He was fourteen and at a Halloween concert in La Flor, Texas. He saw a young girl in a nurse's costume. They sat and talked and drank cokes. She wasn't very pretty, she had some pimples on her face, but he didn't care, she was pleasant. She had a beautiful smile, bright blue eyes and beneath that golden blonde hair, she appeared to have a brain. She talked and made sense to him.

The dream continued. He was graduating from military school. He had done well and was a cadet officer. He needed a date for the graduation prom. He wrote her, she accepted and came. He remembered her name, it was Mary, Mary . . . something? He dozed off.

"Lieutenant," a voice said, "Are you awake?"

"Yes," he replied, "I am now!"

"I'm your Doctor. You've sustained a number of shrapnel wounds. If you are to see again, we need to remove shrapnel from your head and relieve the pressure on the nerves controlling your sight. We believe we'll be successful. We will also remove as much shrapnel from other parts of your body as we can today."

He heard no more. The dream went on. Mary was coming to the prom. He had not seen her since he left Buckshot's ranch. What had happened to Buckshot and Aunt Betsy? He hoped they were well and enjoying their twins.

Mary arrived at the prom. She floated onto the dance floor like a goddess from heaven. She was so beautiful in her black evening gown.

"Lieutenant, are you going to sleep forever? The surgery is over and we are going to remove the bandages from your eyes. Can you move your right arm? Try now to do this." This time the voice was feminine and soft. The bandages came off and the light was blinding. He could see light! The right arm moved much better than before.

He smiled. Everything was fuzzy. "Could I have a drink of water, please?" he said.

"Certainly," she replied and gave him a sip of water.

"Do you think you can hold the cup?" she asked, "Let's see you try!"

He tried but was unsuccessful. She was coming into better focus now. When he closed his left eye he could see her more clearly. He read the name on her white uniform. It said Lt. M.A. Boone.

"Is your name MA Boone or Mister Boone?" he asked, "everything is blurred."

She laughed, "It's M.A. Boone. The M.A. stands for Mary Ann. You are First Lieutenant J.L. Hall, is that correct?"

"Yes ma'am," he answered. "My friends just call me Tex!"

"Where in Texas are you from?" she asked.

"Well, I was born in Austin, but I'm not from Texas now, not since I joined the Marine Corps. Where are you from, Mary Ann?"

"I'm from Texas too," she replied. "My folks have a ranch north of Del Rio, about halfway between Del Rio and the little town of La Flor. To be honest, I've known who you were from the moment you came aboard this ship. It's me, Tex, Mary—Mary Boone from La Flor. Remember, you invited me to your senior prom? I am so glad to see you, and I will do all I can to help you get well, old friend!"

"Oh Mary! Mary Boone, I'm so glad to see you too!"

"Knock it off you two," growled a grizzled voice from the adjacent bed, "keep this up and I'll probably cry!"

"The day that happens, First Sergeant, will be the day the sun rises in the west!" responded Mary, happily.

"Tex, she added, "I do have some good news for you. We'll be airlifting you and some of the other wounded back to the states in a few days. You'll be going to the Balboa Naval Hospital, near San Diego. That'll be the end of my tour aboard this ship as well." She paused slightly, "My orders are also to Balboa Hospital. I'll be in charge of physical therapy there, so I imagine we'll see a lot of each other."

Tex with a hope filled smiled said "That is something I'm looking forward to Nurse Boone!"

"Semper Fi! Marine," laughed Mary, "Semper Fi!"[1]

-The End-

---

[1] *Semper Fi - shortened version of Marine Corps motto Semper Fidelis, meaning always faithful*

CHARACTERS

Jake Hall—Age 13, later "Little Tex"
Jesse Steel—Later "Buckshot"
Betsy Steel—His wife
Snickers—The tan and white dog
Tommy Steel—Deceased
Jim Rivers—Store keeper
Ruth Rivers—His wife and sister of Betsy Steel
Kathy Rivers—Their 13 year old daughter
Timmy Rivers—Their 6 year old son
Star—Betsy Steel's pinto horse
Matilda—The pig which Tex claimed as his pet
Grey—Jesse's number one horse
Black—Jesse's number two horse
Brownie—The pack horse
Oscar—A Belgian sheep dog
Mikey—The boy from the merry-go-round incident
Lee Mitchell—La Flor Sheriff
Will 'Fuzzy' Tinker—Former bank robber, and town's street cleaner
Henry Bryan—La Flor Judge
Doc Hammerstein—Pharmacist and Drug Store owner
Reverend Joshua Creedon—Protestant minister
Norman Cabot—Wealthy newcomer Rancher
Reggie Cabot—Cabot's 16 year old son
Shorty Scrogs—Former Lincoln Brigade soldier and laborer
Bull—Former Lincoln Brigade soldier and laborer
Doctor Simons—La Flor town doctor
Mary Boone—Kathy's friend
"Lonesome" Pine—Sheriff Lee's deputy

AUTHOR'S POSTSCRIPT

Since the early days of my youth, I have enjoyed good cowboy stories and cowboy movies. The format for these classic tales is simple, good and evil forces engage in a struggle and the good always prevails. In my day, the good cowboys wore white hats and rode white horses, while the bad cowboys wore black.

In 1938 branding was widely used to help identify an owner's cattle. The most humane brands were those in which all ends of the brand were open. A closed, or circular configuration created a large scar and usually caused the hair to fall out of the center. This is a reason the Steel's in this story used an "S->", (S-Arrow), brand. The practice of branding cattle with irons is not in universal use these days. Nowadays tattoos and ear tags have replaced branding on many ranches and farms.

While all their works were classified as fiction, the masters of cowboy stories used personal experiences as a basis for their creations. This made stories by Zane Grey, Conrad Richter, Louis L'Amour and Ernest Hemingway, for example, more believable and interesting to the reader. Accordingly, *Buckshot and the Boy* is a fictional cowboy story cast in a believable context. It is built upon some experiences I had on a ranch near Del Rio, Texas, owned by two wonderful people, Herman and Becky Sparks. Matilda the pig was one of the Sparks' hogs and the story of the skunk is based on an event that actually happened. The total content of the story is fictional and was from similar experiences that several friends had, or from stories told by the Marines with whom I once served.

There were a number of friends and family members who helped and encouraged me in this effort. For their support, my thanks and appreciation goes to each and every one of them. I especially wish to thank my wife, Sara, for her patience and for typing the first draft of this story from my handwritten notes. I am extremely proud of and appreciative for the hard work that my granddaughter Kirsten Boyd put forth in typing and editing the text. The help and support from my daughters Linda Bassert, Diana Boyd and Dale Cirillo was outstanding. Many thanks to Mary Hilgartner, Guy and Marie Shaffer, Trent and Gilda Shaver, Bill and Cheryl Banta, LaVonne Gysan, Heidi Kunec, Lindsay Lowell and Andrew Pendergrass, our Great Falls librarian, for their comments and support.

I thank Hilda Griffith who not only helped in the story review process, but also introduced me to Carolyn Chapman. Additionally, this effort would not have been successful without the help of my friend Sam Ginder, who not only advised me on this story, but co-authored our award-winning book, *Highpockets' War Stories and Other Tall Tales*.

My son, David Hilgartner, provided the sketch map of La Flor and the design concept for the book cover. My good friend, W.E. Ten Eyck, developed and drew the book cover using David's concept. I deeply appreciate David's and Bill's assistance.

I cannot leave out my son, Paul Christian Hilgartner, who provided the inspiration for the character "Fuzzy" Tinker in the story. Many thanks, Paul!

I wish to express my appreciation to The Reverend Paul F. Gysan, Pastor of Christ the King Lutheran Church, Great Falls, Virginia, for his support on this story and his comments on the cover. I also wish to thank Carolyn Chapman of the Annandale Ranch for her review and comments on the cover. Last but not least, I wish to thank Mike Swineford for his good natured help in typing the final manuscript drafts of this story, and Bart Edelen for his review of them.

God has blessed me in every way. I hope all who read this story, learn from and enjoy it as much as I did writing it.

Pete Hilgartner

AUTHOR'S BIOGRAPHY

"Highpockets" with his beloved fox-red Labrador retriever, Ruby

Peter L. Hilgartner, a retired U.S. Marine Colonel, was born in Austin, Texas. His father, an eye doctor, owned a ranch near Yorktown, Texas. As a youth, young Hilgartner had the opportunity to experience life on this ranch. Additionally, he spent six months on the southwest Texas ranch owned by Herman and Becky Sparks. The story *Buckshot and The Boy* is a blend of those experiences, as well as the experiences of his brothers and close friends.

As a Marine, he is a veteran of both Korean and Vietnam Wars. In Vietnam, he commanded the 1st Battalion, 5th Marine Regiment earning the nickname from his men of Highpockets, due to his unusual height of 6' 6". He is co-author of *Highpocket's War Stories and Other Tall Tales*, a book which received the 2005 Marine Corps Gazette's Frances Fox Parry Award for the best combat initiative story written in the past two years.

A 1951 graduate of the U.S. Naval Academy, Colonel Hilgartner holds an advanced degree in business management from the U.S. Naval Postgraduate School in Monterey, California. He is an avid outdoorsman and hunter. He is a certified volunteer Senior Hunter Education Instructor with the Virginia Department of Game and Inland Fisheries outreach courses.

Hilgartner and his wife, Sara, and their four dogs reside in Great Falls, Virginia, on the outskirts of Washington, DC, where they enjoy daily adventures exploring God's creation.

BVG